DAY OF REBELLION

The Jack Christie Adventures – Book 4

JOHNNY O'BRIEN

Praise for the Jack Christie Books

"Johnny O'Brien's original and consistently exciting novel makes sure that history truly comes alive in an unforgettable way."
– Nick Tucker, Children's Book Reviewer for the Independent.

"If you're still wondering, may I say that if ever there was a book to take a chance on, this is it. Expect it to win awards, it's that good."
– Amazon reviewer

"The characters of Jack Christie and Angus are brilliantly drawn... you'll visualise the scenes and almost smell them as Jack tries to make sense of his new world. A very satisfying, sometimes shocking, but ultimately uplifting read."
– loverreading.co.uk

"Joy! We love Mr O'Brien! Sam overwhelmed with enthusiasm for the book- desperate to read constantly"
– Kate, Parent, Manchester

"A thrilling war-time adventure that is a perfect mix of historical fact and fictional adventure... this debut novelist has created a real page-turner"
- Julia Eccleshare, lovereadingforkids.co.uk

"History has never been so exciting... Fast-paced and full of action, this is the perfect read for the PlayStation generation"
- Newbooks Magazine

"A suspenseful and entertaining journey... Jack Christie is a very relatable hero... His latest adventure delivers on all counts!"
- Teenreads.co.uk

"In simplest terms, it is a hugely enjoyable adventure story. However, there is much more to this story than just another time-travel adventure. Johnny…manages to weave his story seamlessly in with the actual events and real-life personalities of the time"
- bookzone4boys.blogspot.com

By Johnny O'Brien

Day of the Assassins
(The Jack Christie Adventures – Book 1)

Day of Deliverance
(The Jack Christie Adventures – Book 2)

Day of Vengeance
(The Jack Christie Adventures – Book 3)

Day of Rebellion
(The Jack Christie Adventures – Book 4)

For Sally, Tom, Peter and Anna
- J. O'B.

PROLOGUE
- JACK'S ADVENTURES SO FAR...

It has been several months since Jack and his friend, Angus, discovered that their school in Soonhope in the Borders of Scotland, is a front for a secret team of scientists, called 'VIGIL', who control the most powerful technology ever conceived: the technology of time travel. At the heart of this technology is a machine called the Taurus, which controls 'time phones' used by time travellers to move from one historical period to another. Jack's father, Professor Tom Christie, led the team that originally built the Taurus. However, having perfected the machine, Christie's team had a fatal disagreement and Christie was forced into exile, leaving Jack and his mother, Carole, in Soonhope.

Professor Christie's plan was to use time travel to make changes in the past that would alter the future for the better. He had big ideas – like going back in time to stop entire wars from starting in the first place. He attracted passionate supporters from the original Taurus team, including Dr Pendelshape, Jack's old history teacher. Pendelshape, Christie and their small band of followers called themselves 'Revisionists'. They used computer simulations to help plan the changes they wanted to make in the past in order to change or 'revise' the future. But others from Christie's original Taurus team believed that changing events in the past, however well meant, was dangerous because it was impossible to fully predict the consequences. They formed a separate group – called 'VIGIL' – to ensure that the Taurus and the ability to time travel was kept a very closely guarded secret. They housed the Taurus machine in an underground complex beneath the school in Soonhope. Today the teachers have ordinary jobs at the school, which acts as a front for VIGIL, and second lives as VIGIL agents.

Jack and Angus became embroiled in the conflict between VIGIL and the Revisionists when, unknown to VIGIL, Tom Christie and the Revisionists secretly created a second Taurus. Using plans drawn up from their computer simulations, the Revisionists used their Taurus to go back in time to try and stop the First World War – saving millions of lives and changing the course of history. But VIGIL got wind of the plans and managed to stop them. Jack and Angus found themselves caught between VIGIL and the Revisionists, and Jack's loyalties were torn. In the end, having witnessed the dangers of time travel and intervening in the past in order to change the future, Jack decided that the right thing to do was to side with VIGIL, even though this meant he was unlikely to see his father again.

Having failed in their first attempt to intervene in history and so change the future, the Revisionists made two further attempts to change the past. The first of these was in Elizabethan England and the second was in 1940 – during the early part of the Second World War. As a result of these events, Pendelshape, who by now had become leader of the Revisionists, was killed, and the Revisionists were finally defeated by VIGIL. Tom Christie survived, however, and a reconciliation is now underway between him and his old colleagues at VIGIL. Tom has seen how intervening in the past might have tragic consequences and also recognises how much his actions and those of Pendelshape and the other Revisionists have endangered his own family. However, relations have not yet thawed sufficiently for him to return to VIGIL, or to his family in Soonhope.

In their last adventure in 1940, Jack and Angus were forced to leave a VIGIL time phone in 1940s London on top of Nelson's Column in Trafalgar Square. VIGIL agents are now planning to recover it, in case it falls into the wrong hands…

CHAPTER 1
- THE SUMMER PALACE

Beijing, China, 1860

Jack was speechless. Stretching before him was an astonishing fairy-tale world of gardens, lakes, fountains and pavilions. There were hundreds of structures – all of them extraordinarily beautiful. But the peace was temporary. Jack felt a tremor in the earth like a rumbling earthquake. He glanced round. A whole posse of Imperial cavalry had spotted the two of them and were hurtling towards them through the gardens. "Come on!" Angus screamed.

He led them off the main path and into a narrow, hedged passageway. Beyond, there was a wide, grass bank, which rose gently in front of the most astonishing building they had yet seen – a miniature palace. But there was no time to stand and admire it. They climbed up the marble steps and through the lavish entrance, dashed inside and into a long, vast hallway. Lining one side were a series of huge jade vases. They were twice Jack's height and yet so delicate and thin the light shone straight through them.

They paused for breath halfway along the hall. "What now?" Jack said, his chest heaving.

For the first time, Angus did not seem to know what to do or where to go.

Suddenly, there was a loud crash behind them. They wheeled round. A huge cavalryman sat astride a muscular black horse at the end of the great hall. He had ridden up the steps and into the pavilion. His steel helmet glimmered and its long, feathered plume quivered. The horse bucked, and the cavalryman balanced his lance in his right hand, digging his heels hard into the flanks of his horse. It reared… and then it charged. The horseman skilfully manoeuvred the lance, angling it towards Jack and Angus. Jack dived for cover, but Angus was too slow. Crying out in horror as the lance pierced his friend's chest, Jack raced to where Angus lay slumped on the floor and cradled his head in his hands. It lolled back uselessly, his eyes staring up to the gilded rafters above. Fired up with rage, Jack leaped up, reaching for the sword at his belt. But the lancer was already well into his second charge. The horse snorted as it thundered at him and all Jack could do was stare down the shaft of the lance as its cold steel tip entered his chest, just below his heart.

CHAPTER 2
- CONTACT

"That Lancer Boss is impossible to get past," Angus threw his controller away in disgust.

"I know… but what do you think?" Jack glanced away from the screen with its frozen image of Jack and Angus prostrate on the marble floor of the Yuan Ming Yuan Haiyan. It was one of the most extraordinary buildings ever constructed and the makers of *Point-of-Departure – Day of Rebellion, China 1860* had lovingly brought it to life as accurately as they could.

Angus inspected the plastic games case.

"It's good. Multiplayer is awesome. Those big battle scenes with the Chinese Imperials against the Taiping rebels …"

"Bit different to the other POD games. And the alternative history scenarios, I've got to say, they're brilliant." Jack smiled. "You know why that is, don't you?"

Angus scooped up a huge handful of popcorn and stuffed it into his mouth, "No – why?" He spat half of the popcorn back out of his mouth as he spoke.

"That's nice." Jack tried to ignore it. "I found out something very interesting yesterday. I was called into VIGIL – they wanted me to go through the whole Second World War thing with them again…"

Angus rolled his eyes, "What? We've been through it, like, a billion times already."

Jack shrugged. "You know what they're like. They're worried about the time phone…"

"What – the one you left up on top of Nelson's Column?"

"Yes."

"Well, it was a pretty stupid thing to do… I mean leaving a working time phone back in 1940… unlike you to mess up like that, Jack. You must feel pretty bad – putting the whole of the human race at risk…" Angus shook his head.

"Thanks for that. You might remember, we were under a bit of pressure at the time, and anyway I don't recall you being much use – you just jumped off."

"I'm winding you up," Angus narrowed his eyes as he relived his BASE-jumping experience from the top of Nelson's Column "But you've got to admit, it was pure adrenaline. And the look on your face as you hit the ground… priceless!"

"Hilarious," Jack deadpanned. "Anyway, VIGIL is still going on about it. I think they're going to send an agent to get the time phone. As you say, it's not ideal for it to just sit there…"

"Must be a bit rusty by now too. Who will they send to get it?"

Jack shrugged, "Tony… Gordon – one of the happy couple probably."

"Good luck to them. Anyway, you were going to tell me something."

"Oh yeah, you won't believe this, but guess who's really behind Point-of-Departure?"

Angus flipped the games case over in his hand, "Dunno. Some evil global corporation?"

Jack cleared his throat. "Nope – the world-famous POD series – biggest game series of all time, with huge global sales and its first film coming out next year, belongs to VIGIL."

"What?"

"It's VIGIL. VIGIL is behind POD!"

Angus looked stunned, "But…"

"Inchquin told me yesterday when I was up at VIGIL HQ," Jack explained. "He thought it was funny that we've played all the different games, and we never knew. It makes sense though, doesn't it? All the historical stuff – super accurate with all the alternative histories caused by different things you could do in the past… only VIGIL would have the knowledge to design a game like that."

Angus was agog. "Wow! I never thought… but… why would they do that?"

"Easy. They can make money out of it. Loads of money. It can't be cheap keeping VIGIL going, so they've built up a nice little side-line in software and gaming."

Angus shook his head and stared at the screen. "You're right – all this – it's a bit like the stuff we've seen in the Timeline Simulator. Yeah, it makes sense."

"And, believe it or not, Inchquin said that Dad wrote some of the original software years ago, when he was at CERN with Mum. The algorithms used in VIGIL's Timeline Simulator are apparently quite similar to the ones they've used in the POD games – you know, for the alternative histories. They were way ahead of their time."

"Must have been nice for them, coding together, the happy nerds," Angus grinned.

"Anyway, do you want to have another shot – see if we can get past that cavalry guy?"

But as Jack picked up the controller and turned his attention back to the screen, something odd happened.

The frozen image of Jack and Angus dead on the floor of the Chinese palace disappeared and the screen went completely black. "Uh-oh…" Jack got up to approach the console, but then stopped in his tracks.

The black screen flickered and then, from the top left, a message appeared.

Msg from timetraveller01: Hope you guys are enjoying the new game. Sorry to disturb you. I have made some decisions. They affect us all. For now I don't want VIGIL involved. Small steps first. Short notice, I know, but would like to meet at the Edinburgh Museum at

2 p.m. this afternoon. Just you two. I will explain everything when we meet. Nothing to worry about, but make sure you come alone.

There was another flicker of the screen as the mysterious message signed off, with one final word:

Dad.

CHAPTER 3
– MEMORIES OF HEAVEN

"What does it mean?" Jack stared at the screen. "Your dad wants to see us. Sounds like he's been doing some thinking. Cool way to get in touch, eh? Through the game."

"But…"

"Come on." Angus looked at his watch. "It's half twelve. I've got a spare helmet. We can be there in less than an hour."

"I don't know what he wants…"

"And if you don't go you never will."

"What about Mum?"

"She's out – right?"

"Yeah – she was going on about making sure we shut the door and locked up if we went anywhere."

"Well, she doesn't need to know, and that's how your dad wants it." Angus was already climbing back up the stairs from Jack's cellar. He stopped halfway up and turned back to Jack who was still staring dumbfounded at the screen.

"Come on. It'll be fine. In fact, this could be it – your dad's plan to finally end the fight with VIGIL… Maybe he's going to come home."

Jack followed Angus up the stairs. His mind was so preoccupied that he forgot to turn off the console and the message from 'timetraveller01' lingered on the screen behind them.

Jack clambered onto the back of the bike – Angus had 'borrowed' his dad's KTM – and they powered up the old drive from Cairnfield. It was a fine summer's day and soon they were racing their way through the countryside towards Edinburgh, with Jack still trying to make meaning of his dad's strange message. He was nervous but exhilarated. It was less than a month since Jack and Angus had travelled back from 1940. With his dad's help they had prevented a Revisionist attempt to intervene in World War Two from going disastrously wrong. They had also saved VIGIL from defeat by the Revisionists. It had been a close-run thing. Jack should have felt elated at the result, but actually he was in a state of limbo. Things which should have been sorted out still weren't. Pendelshape was dead and they believed that the Revisionists had been destroyed; for a moment it had seemed that his dad would be reconciled with his old colleagues, Inchquin, the Rector and the rest of VIGIL. Jack had witnessed a moment of tenderness between his mum and dad and had fleetingly hoped they might get back together. But then, at the final moment, his dad had decided that it was all too much, too soon, and he couldn't come back... yet. It had been back to square one.

But now this strange message had arrived, only a few weeks later. So maybe Angus was right and his father had finally made up his mind. The Revisionists' attempts to intervene in history to control the future had failed, but more than that, they had almost wiped themselves out in the process. With Pendelshape dead and many, maybe all, of the other Revisionists either dead or captured by VIGIL, perhaps his dad had finally decided enough was enough; and it was time to come in from the cold.

Two giant warriors stood either side of the entrance to the museum. The models were very lifelike. One was dressed in a red jacket, blue trousers and boots. He wore light leather and metal armour on his top half. His helmet had leather chin straps and he was carrying a huge black banner. Jack read a small plaque beside the figure:

TAIPING REBELLION WOMEN'S INFANTRY – 1855

He did a double take as he realised that the figure was not a man but a replica figure of a female warrior. Opposite, there was an equally ferocious Chinese soldier carrying a green flag. His plaque read:

IMPERIAL (QING DYNASTY) INFANTRY – 1855

Ahead, above the information desk to the museum, there was a large banner:

MEMORIES OF HEAVEN
The Heavenly Kingdom comes to Edinburgh
Welcome to the Taiping Experience

"Do you think this is Dad trying to be funny?" Jack asked.
"Why?" said Angus.
"This… big China exhibition thing. China in the mid-nineteenth century – Taiping rebellion, Opium Wars, all that…"
"What about it?"
Jack sighed, "It's the same as the game, the new Point-of-Departure – Day of Rebellion." Jack tapped his temple with his index finger. "Duh. It's all the same period of history. Dad knew we were playing POD China and so he thought it would be funny to meet us here where they've got a big exhibition about it."
"Oh right… I get you," Angus said, then grimaced. "Do I?" Jack shook his head in despair. "Anyway, what do we do? Just hang around for him?"
"He'll probably be keeping a low profile. I suppose we should wander around."

They approached the front desk where a young assistant was pointing a couple towards the far end of the huge atrium, "… introductory lectures are in the open area at the end of the hall there, then there's a guided tour of the main China exhibit. The guide is just starting one now…" The woman nodded towards the far end of the hall where people were seated in rows in front of a screen.

Jack shrugged, "Might as well take a look…"

As they moved through the main hall towards the presentation, they could already hear the amplified voice of the guide talking to the group.

"… the Taiping Rebellion in China was the second bloodiest war of any kind in history," she announced. As she spoke a series of images were scrolling by on the big screen behind her. There were pictures of great throngs of soldiers holding black flags, Chinese cities with amazing architecture, astounding works of art, peasants at work in fields… The guide kept talking: "Some estimate that the total number of deaths during the Taiping Rebellion, between 1850 and 1864, may have exceeded thirty million. That's three times as many as died in the First World War. Yet, in the West, few have even heard of the Taiping Rebellion…"

"Do we really want to listen to this?" Angus sighed. "I mean, people talking about history is OK and everything, but they should really ask the experts – people who've actually been there. Like me."

Jack smiled and tuned in to the guide's talk.

"There were many amazing things about the Taiping people, and their enemies – China's ruling Qing dynasty. Take, for example, Taiping rebellion's leader, Hong Xiuquan—" the guide paused and a line drawing of a Chinese man in an elaborately embroidered robe and an ornate hat appeared on the screen. "It is said that Hong Xiuquan fell into a trance and saw visions of heaven that inspired him to overthrow the Qing. He and his followers practised their own version of Christianity, and because the Taiping were Christians, they attracted some European support. For a while the Taiping were very successful. They had a good army and they moved north, eventually taking the city of Nanjing in 1853. But the rebellion left China weak and open to exploitation by the British, French and others…"

The guide droned on and after a while Jack found his attention wavering. With the words, "Now, let me welcome you to the Heavenly Kingdom – and the Taiping Experience…" she suddenly stopped talking and the screen rose upwards, revealing two large glass doors which swung open to allow visitors into the dimly lit exhibition areas. The crowd drifted forward.

Jack nudged Angus, who was gazing distractedly at the floor. "We're on."

It was an impressive exhibition. There were intricately patterned silk costumes of all shapes and sizes. Then there was a full model layout of the Third Battle of Nanjing with an Imperial army assault on the city battlements. It was all laid out in miniature with row upon row of soldiers, cannons and cavalry. The city was being defended by the Taiping – in their red jackets and blue trousers. Further down the exhibition hall, there were more figures, this time representing the Taiping's enemy – the Imperialist Qing. There was a bit on punishment and torture, including photographs of 'slow slicing', where a series of precise incisions cut away the victim's flesh before he was left to die.

Suddenly, Jack felt himself being jostled by the crowd behind. He half turned in irritation and felt something thrust into his hands. It was an envelope. He scanned the faces behind him but whoever who had delivered the envelope had already slipped away into the throng.

CHAPTER 4
- TANTALLON

Jack barged through the crowd out of the gloom of the exhibition hall and into the light of the atrium. He ripped open the envelope. Inside, there was a single sheet of folded paper. It read:

Meet you at Tantallon

"What does that mean?" Angus said, finally catching up with Jack and peering over his shoulder. "Did you see who gave it to you?"

Jack looked anxiously around the museum, but it was just the same scene of visitors and tourists quietly milling around. The mystery contact had vanished into thin air.

"He's gone." Jack stared at the piece of paper. "Didn't even see him. Was it Dad?"

"No – he wouldn't have just left. Anyway, what's Tantallon?" Angus pressed.

"It's a castle on the coast... Mum and Dad used to take me there when I was a kid."

Angus gunned the KTM due east and the Edinburgh suburbs peeled away into the East Lothian countryside which spread out from the bare, rolling hills of the Lammermuirs down to the grey-blue sea of the Firth of Forth. It was a fine day, but Jack worried about what they would find when they arrived.

He reached into his pocket and pulled out his VIGIL smart device. He'd lost the previous model in Paris in 1940, but VIGIL was issuing new devices to all their personnel. Jack had received his the day before at VIGIL and Angus was fed up that his own had not yet arrived. The device looked like a smart phone and it gave the user access to all sorts of apps. But it also gave VIGIL agents access to a number of special VIGIL applications about history, technology, inventions and most fields of human endeavour. It was like having a whole encyclopaedia in a little box and, for any VIGIL agent called on another time-travel mission, it would be invaluable.

Jack had shown Angus an amazing VIGIL app that had detailed descriptions of how things worked, with technical drawings, cutaways and animations of different car and bike engines, aeroplanes and just about anything you could think of. The app also showed how these technologies had developed over time. It was important for VIGIL to understand, study and record such things, so they knew how things fit together and their impact on history. Right now though, Jack was only interested in the device's sat nav, which he was using to guide Angus towards Tantallon.

An hour later they were well into the countryside and had turned off an isolated coast road onto a dirt track. It was a flat, treeless landscape and there was no one around. They could see the sea in the distance and smell the fresh salt air.

After ten minutes, they pulled up to a simple wooden shack built next to a small turning circle.

"There." Jack said.

There was a rusty sign next to the shack:

TANTALLON CASTLE

"Not much of a castle."

"That's not it. That's where you get in. The castle is further on." Jack looked around and took off his helmet. The breeze ruffled his hair. "I remember it now. It's ages since I was here."

They walked towards the shack.

"Can't believe there's anyone in there." Angus knocked on the window of the shack. Inside they could see an assortment of yellowing postcards, a few souvenirs and a mouldy fridge with some soft drinks way past their sell-by date.

Angus knocked again. "Anyone at home?"

Suddenly a head popped up from behind the counter and the window slid open. Angus jumped. The attendant was old and grey and he had a pipe in one hand which he rested on the counter. He stared at them with beady eyes.

"On your own?" He looked at them suspiciously and then craned his head out of the shack to check there was no one else around.

"Yes..."

"Follow the track up to the castle." He nodded at the bike. "You'll have to leave that here. And you'll need this." He handed them a small package. "Go to the pit prison. It's inside the castle; you'll find it easy enough. Only open the package when you're down there. Don't worry, there's no other visitors today..." he flashed a toothless grin. "Like most days."

"But..."

"Go!" The man hissed and he slammed the window shut and the hut shook.

"Polite here, aren't they?" Angus said.

They opened an old gate next to the hut and set off down a track through a mown field. Ahead was a vast, grassy rampart. Jack and Angus rounded the rampart and suddenly there it was – a massive ruined castle. In fact, it looked less like a castle and more like a solid wall of red sandstone. It towered over twenty metres into the sky and extended across a large promontory hanging over the sea.

"Impressive."

"Yeah. Beyond that huge wall there is just some land which juts out to sea. There are cliffs on all the other sides. But I don't get it – why has Dad sent us here – where is he anyway?"

"Yeah – why not just meet us at the museum?" Angus said. "Maybe he's still afraid we'd be followed or something.

Maybe he'll be waiting for us in the pit dungeon, or whatever it's called. We'd better try to find it."

Suddenly, a worrying thought flashed into Jack's head. What if the note hadn't been from his dad at all...?

"Pit prison – sounds pleasant. Look – there's a plan of the castle on that sign."

They crossed the drawbridge over the ditch at the front of the castle and passed through the gate into the central courtyard. There were breathtaking views out to sea, which sparkled in the sunlight.

"Look at that."

Angus pointed at a huge rock rising vertically from the water only about a mile out from the castle.

"That's the Bass Rock. It's an island. I remember going around it in a boat once. Nearly threw up. You should see it close up – the cliffs are incredible. It's got a lighthouse. See?"

"People live on it?"

"No. I think there used to be a prison... would have been impossible to escape. Come on – this hanging around is making me nervous."

They entered the ruined state rooms at the west end of the castle site.

"Down here..."

"You going to open that package now?"

"The old guy said to open it when we got down there."

Jack could scarcely see his way as they stepped from ground level and brilliant sunlight into the dank bowels of the castle. They descended a steep spiral staircase before finally reaching a small room. A single electric bulb up on the wall gave off a faint light. The room was empty.

"Grim. Is this it?" Angus asked.

Jack nodded. "Time to open the package."

He peeled back layers of brown paper and out slipped a thin plastic object. His heart jumped when he saw it and he glanced knowingly at Angus.

"Interesting. Looks just like a VIGIL access device. You going to give it a go?"

Jack's thumb twitched on the device and suddenly a small opening appeared in the floor beneath Angus's feet.

Angus jumped aside, "Whoa!"

Where Angus had been standing, there was a circular metal covering set in a concrete base. It looked a bit like a drain cover.

Jack pressed the device a second time and the metal cover slid open to reveal a hole in the ground. It led to a steeply raked spiral staircase.

Angus gawped. "Identical to the VIGIL entry portals."

"Yeah. But I don't think this one goes anywhere near VIGIL. I think it goes somewhere else altogether."

CHAPTER 5
- SUB-SEA

A s they walked onto the spiral staircase, the steps began lowering automatically and the aperture closed silently above their heads. After a few minutes of descent they came to a gentle halt. Ahead of them was a door. Jack pressed the device again and the door opened into a short metal-clad corridor lit by a dim blue glow. At the end of the corridor was a circular metal door. Jack and Angus exchanged glances.

"I'm assuming your dad intends us to keep going…"

"Incredible – everything's just like VIGIL." But then Jack noticed that the door did not have the familiar 'VIGIL' logo etched onto it. Instead, there was a phrase:

Change the Past. Save the Future.

The door opened without a sound, revealing a long tubular passageway which melted into the darkness. The passage walls at the VIGIL complex were brilliantly engineered – completely smooth with no rivets and no seams. But this place was different. The passage was hewn directly from the rock. Water dripped down from above and every few metres the roof was supported by old and rusty steel struts. It was like a badly maintained mineshaft.

"This tunnel has got to go right under the sea."

"It's giving me the creeps… and it all looks pretty rickety.

Are we just going to go on?" Angus said.

"What the...?" Jack jumped as, suddenly, a small open car appeared out of the gloom and glided to a halt right in front of them.

"It's on rails..."

"Nearly gave me a heart attack... it's just like a ghost train."

"It must be automatic. Do you reckon we just get in?"

Soon they were trundling through the claustrophobic tunnel and after a few minutes the mysterious rail car came to a halt next to a low concrete platform.

"Guess this is it, then."

"I don't get it, Jack. I mean, why isn't your dad here to meet us? It's almost like he's set us a weird test or something."

Jack gave a shrug and looked around. "What now?"

"Maybe we go down there – it looks like there's some sort of lift?"

At one end of the platform a mesh cage rose up from the ground and directly into the roof. They approached it and Jack craned his head upwards.

"It's just a big black hole – can't see a thing, which is really weird, because I swear the tunnel was going in the direction of the sea. I don't get how we're not underwater now – that hole just seems to go up."

"Maybe it's the Bass Rock," Angus said. "Maybe we've gone under the sea and now we're under the rock itself. Look – there's a button. Shall I give it a go?"

Jack nodded. Angus pressed the button and there was a mechanical whirring from above.

"Well, something's working up there..."

They waited with bated breath as they heard the lift cage rattling down the shaft from above. Suddenly, the bottom of the yellow-painted metal cage appeared and jolted to a halt in front of them. Jack's heart missed a beat.

Inside the lift cage was a man, with his back turned to them, leaning heavily against the latticed door. Without warning, the door slid open and the man tumbled out, slumping over the access gate.

He didn't move. Jack and Angus rushed forward. The man's head fell back, his eyes stared unblinking at the tunnel roof.

Jack's heart was racing. He peered closer and then turned to Angus, his face etched with fear.

"God Angus – he's dead. Looks like he's been shot." They laid the man out onto the platform.

"Who is he?"

Jack shook his head. "No idea."

"What are we going to do?"

Jack felt his chest thumping. "Dad. He must be up there. Maybe there's been some sort of fight… maybe he's in trouble. I think we need to go up."

"Hold on, Jack, is that clever? Maybe we should go back… get help… get VIGIL here."

"But what about Dad?"

"Jack – we don't even know if it was really your dad who sent the message… maybe it's a trick…"

"Well, I'm going up – you can go back if you want."

They climbed into the cage. There were three buttons, one above the other:

Ground Exit

Complex

Top Exit – Rock

"What do you reckon? I'm going to try Complex." Jack pushed the button.

There was a jolt and the cage started to ascend through the lift shaft hewn into the rock. Minutes later the cage came to a halt with a lurch. Jack pulled back the gate and they stepped into a narrow tunnel. After a few metres they arrived at another metal doorway.

"Guess this must be it. Entrance to the 'Complex'. Whatever that is."

"Try the access device on this door. But get ready – we don't know what's behind it."

The door opened and for a moment there was just pitch darkness. Then, one by one, lights started to flicker on.

Jack and Angus stood dumbfounded at the scene before them.

The room was similar to the underground library at Jack's house in Cairnfield. It was oval shaped and there were books and papers on shelves and stacked up everywhere. There were all sorts of paraphernalia on display in various glass cabinets.

Angus found his voice. "This is it, isn't it? It's the Revisionist base. What VIGIL would give to see this."

"Buried somewhere beneath the Bass Rock in the middle of the Firth of Forth... mind blowing," Jack said. "How did they build it all?"

"And keep it secret?"

Jack bit his lip. "It's like the *Marie Celeste*."

"Yeah – too creepy."

Jack stepped further into the library and suddenly stopped in his tracks. He felt his insides convulse.

"Oh God... there's another one."

CHAPTER 6
- THE ROCK

The second body was lying face up next to a low table in the library. The man's lifeless eyes stared at the ceiling and a dark pool of blood oozed out from beneath him. Jack's shock was tempered by only one thing. The body wasn't his father's.

"That blood looks fresh... it must have just happened." Jack didn't want to look any closer.

Angus pointed to the floor. "You're right, dark drops... it's a trail of blood... goes through to the next room."

"Must be from that guy..."

"No. Look. It stops well before where he's lying. Someone else must be injured."

Jack trembled in horror. "It could be Dad's blood."

Suddenly, from deep inside the underground complex, they heard a dull mechanical whine. It was rising quickly in pitch and volume, like a jet engine preparing for take-off.

Jack glanced at Angus. They recognised the noise and knew it meant only one thing.

Without saying a word, they rushed through the doorway at the far end of the library. The scene before them was strangely familiar. Directly in front of them, was a solid wall of thick green glass that extended from the floor all the way up to the ceiling. The glass had the same hue and texture as the Taurus blast screen at VIGIL HQ. Beyond this was a large machine embedded within a network of interconnecting pipes, cables and gantries. They were standing in front of the Revisionist's time-travel machine. It was just like the

VIGIL Taurus, but, if anything, even bigger. Jack and Angus stopped in their tracks and stared in amazement. They could tell by the shrill scream of the generators and the throb of the alert lights that the Taurus was already fully powered up. Jack looked up to the transfer platform in the upper level of the machine. The atmosphere above the platform within the semi-enclosed transfer chamber was changing. It was as if the air had become molten and was moving and wobbling like some sort of super-heated plasma. Up on the platform, Jack could see a man. His image distorted and then, suddenly, he was gone. Almost instantaneously they heard the generators power down and in seconds the Taurus returned to normal.

"That guy up there – I couldn't see clearly – but are you thinking what I'm thinking?" Angus said uneasily.

"I know…" Jack agreed his voice trembling with fear, "it looked just like him…"

"Pendelshape."

"But it's impossible. Pendelshape is dead. We saw it with our own eyes – we saw him die in France in 1940."

"Maybe it was a trick of the light."

Suddenly the blast screen started to lower and in seconds it had encased itself back in its housing. Now Jack and Angus could see the Revisionist Taurus in all its detail. It sat there, brooding and waiting, like some powerful mythical beast.

"What a monster."

"Look…" Angus said, and pointed.

The trail of blood from the library led directly up to the Taurus and onto the steps that accessed the gantry to the transfer platform.

"So it was the guy who was hurt…" Angus said.

"Or maybe someone else…" Angus looked at Jack quizzically. "I don't know, Angus, but there's been a serious fight here. Two guys are dead. Maybe Dad wanted to meet us here but something went badly wrong. Maybe when he got here, he found these guys – I don't know… Maybe they're the last of the Revisionists? Maybe that one we saw up on the transfer platform actually is Pendelshape. When you're meddling with time travel – anything can happen."

"Can't be. It makes no sense… and anyway… where was he going?"

Jack thought for a moment. "That's what I'm saying. It could be they had a fight with Dad and… Dad ended up using the Taurus to escape. That man we saw is going after him. Perhaps it's Dad who's hurt. Maybe badly hurt." Jack turned to Angus his face set in grim determination. "I'm going after him, Angus."

"Hold on – that's nuts. We don't know where they've gone. Anyway, your dad knows how to look after himself."

"Not if he's badly injured." Jack challenged Angus, "You going to help me or not?"

Angus paused and looked back at Jack, "What do you think? Let you go off on your own, getting into trouble and having all the fun. No way. I'm in."

For a split second a smile shaped Jack's lips.

He turned to the Taurus control area. "See there – all those time phones are ready in their pods, but two are missing… if I can get into the system the online activity log should tell me where they've gone…"

Jack tapped at a keyboard. Over the last few months he had become more and more proficient with VIGIL's astonishing technology – and the Revisionist systems seemed to be just the same. He was no expert but he knew enough.

"I've got it… the summary activity log…" His eyes narrowed at the screen, "But I don't get it."

"What?"

"It can't be…"

The information on the recent Taurus time-travel event blinked back at them.

TAURUS ACTIVITY LOG

Departure summary:

Time Phone Serial: 009

Time Phone Holder: Fenton P.
Departure Date: June 23rd 2013 / 2:45 p.m.
Departure Location: Firth of Forth, Scotland.
Arrival summary:
Time Phone Serial: 009
Time Phone Holder: Fenton P.
Arrival Date: July 15th 2046 / 11:23 p.m.
Arrival Location: Firth of Forth, Scotland.

"Fenton P. Is that the name of the guy we saw on the transfer platform…?"

"Could be… but look again… look at his arrival date." Angus peered at the screen. "Well there's the date and time – but, hold on, it says 2046. But that's in…"

Jack finished Angus's sentence, "…the future."

"That's…"

"…impossible?" Jack said.

"You think your dad has modified the Revisionist Taurus so it can transport people to the future?"

"Look, if I scroll down, I should get the previous time-travel event…"

Jack tapped the mouse. "Yes… Look!" He said, triumphantly.

TAURUS ACTIVITY LOG
Departure summary:
Time Phone Serial: 002
Time Phone Holder: Tom C.
Departure Date: June 23rd 2013 / 2:29 p.m.
Departure Location: Firth of Forth, Scotland.
Arrival summary:
Time Phone Serial: 009
Time Phone Holder: Tom C.
Arrival Date: July 14th 2046 / 10:09 p.m.
Arrival Location: Firth of Forth, Scotland.

"This proves Dad was here. There's hardly going to be another Tom C. – and it shows that he left here just before that Fenton guy followed him. Looks like it was a close call. He went to the future – and Fenton followed him there. But that's interesting… the arrival date is different. Dad got there a day earlier."

"Why would that be? I mean, if Fenton was after him, why not arrive before and surprise him?"

"Yeah… it must be the time signal constraints. You know – you can't just go when and where you want. You set the parameters you want and the Taurus is programmed to do its best to meet them. But it tries to avoid people flying repeatedly in and out of the same space and time."

"Armageddon scenario."

"Right. The VIGIL guys say the Taurus tries to manage it, but it's risky. The constraints can vary. Fenton probably got as close as he could to when Dad arrived."

"So now what?"

Jack's brow furrowed as he stared at the screen in front of them. "I think it's pretty obvious, don't you?"

"We'll need some kit… packs, clothing… let's get on it."

Jack's breathing was becoming heavier and his whole nervous system buzzed as if it was wired to the mains. The fact that he had endured this experience several times before did not make him feel any better. Nor was he comforted by the fact that, for the first time, the mighty Taurus would transport them not to the past, but to the future. Or so they hoped. Jack started to notice the physical changes around him in the Taurus chamber as they approached the event horizon – the point of no return. He could hear the shrill scream of the generators, but for some reason the sound was more muffled in their position on the transfer platform high up on the Taurus. Around his feet he could see shimmering eddies of light – the electrical disturbance caused by the temporary wormhole: ion-charged curtains of blue, red and green light. As the shimmering became stronger, it was as if he was standing in the rippling waters of an illuminated whirlpool. The atmosphere within the Taurus structure was also changing and the control room beyond appeared darker and fuzzier. Jack clenched his fists and gritted his teeth…

3… 2… 1

CHAPTER 7
- 2046

The scene before Jack and Angus, from their position on the Taurus transfer platform, seemed little different from the one they had looked out on only seconds before. There was one other important change, however, and it only took Jack a single glance at his time phone to confirm the incredible truth. The readout winked back at him:

Date: July 16th 2046
Time: 2:33 p.m.
Location: Bass Rock, Firth of Forth, Scotland.

2046. That was the important number. The year. It meant they had travelled more than forty years into the future.

"You OK?" Angus said.

"That usual sick feeling. But I'll be alright. The place looks empty – but there seems to be power."

"Yeah. But we can't be too sure."

"Look – the blood trail again..."

Jack pointed to the entry gantry leading off the Taurus transfer platform. The thin spattering of blood, now dried, continued all the way along, then downstairs.

"I guess we follow it and we'll discover something soon enough."

"Or someone... we need to be careful."

Jack studied the time phone readout. "The Taurus has sent us here on 16th July – that's two days after Dad and a day after Fenton."

"Yeah – but we don't know where they've gone. They could still be here. We need to be careful."

The trail of brown-red drops continued into the room below. It then traced its way through to the exit that led back through the library and into a whole separate area of the Revisionist underground complex. The place seemed deserted. There was no sign of Jack's father or the mysterious 'Fenton'. The complex contained a storeroom, kitchen and sleeping quarters. But the trail led them to a small infirmary where it was evident, from some loose bandages and an open bottle of disinfectant, that someone had attempted a hasty patch-up job.

"The blood trail stops here. If it was him, it looks like your dad managed to stem the blood flow."

Jack bit his lip. "That's one conclusion…"

The library was the central hub of the complex and there were a number of further rooms leading off it. One of them was some kind of large laboratory. There were computer terminals everywhere, papers strewn around, whiteboards with diagrams and equations scribbled across them, and lots of scientific equipment. Amongst the mess, Jack caught sight of a few historical artefacts which looked a bit out of place. There was an earthenware pot, some medals and an assortment of old firearms.

"What a mess," Angus said.

"The place looks deserted but something's definitely been happening in here recently. Everything's on standby."

"Yeah – look at those screens over there, they look like CCTV pictures showing bits of the complex. But I can't see any sign of life. And those ones seem to show the outside – see?"

"You're right…" Jack's eyes squinted as he stared at the monitors. "But it's weird, maybe the colour isn't right or something… looks to me like outside, well, it's difficult to make anything out. It's just white."

"Maybe we should go outside and see what's up there?"

"Worth a try."

They entered the lift and Jack pressed the button that said 'Top Exit – Rock'. The contraption groaned and started to shake its way up through the shaft. After a few minutes it slowed.

"You ready?" Angus said.

The lift ground to a halt at the top of the shaft. "There's some sort of access hatch through there."

They clambered up through the hatch into a short passage. "Over there – a door."

"Solid. We're not going to get through that." Angus said.

"Unless..." In his pocket Jack still had the access device which had opened the door from the Tantallon side. Taking it out he pointed it at the door and pressed.

"Works – nice one."

It opened and they were suddenly hit with an icy blast of air. "Geez – that's cold!" Angus said. "Look – more stairs over there."

They climbed up and stepped out in a strange room with curved walls. Ahead was a spiral staircase.

Jack reached out and ran his finger along the wall.

"I think I know where we've come out," he said. "You remember when we were standing at the castle and looking out at the Bass Rock? I think we're inside the lighthouse that we saw built on the rock. Those steps must go right up to the top. Up there we should get a view of everything around. Come on."

They crept forward and slowly climbed the spiral staircase. They could hear nothing except for an occasional breath of wind that caressed the outside of the lighthouse. They reached a door at the top. Jack threw it open and gasped at the sight before them. A few hours before, Jack and Angus had looked out from Tantallon Castle across the mainland, onto a glistening blue-grey sea. It had been a bright summer's day. Now, the view was quite, quite different. They were standing above a desolate landscape of ice and rock. The sea that surrounded the island, and which extended off to the horizon and to the land masses on either side of the Firth of Forth, was completely frozen. It was as if they were looking straight down onto a vast glacier. There was ice and snow everywhere.

The sun blazed out strongly from a cloudless sky and Jack had to squint and then shield his eyes. He stared in disbelief, and then looked at Angus who wore the same expression of shock.

He felt himself starting to panic. "Angus – I don't get it – it was summer when we left, I know we're forty years in the future… but everything's changed… it's like there's been a new ice age or something. The whole world's changed – what's happened?"

CHAPTER 8
- THE RIG

In the distance, far across the smooth landscape of ice, there was a single sign of life. It was a huge steel platform. The structure was supported by pillars but tilted so that half the platform was buried in the surrounding ice. "What is it?" Jack said. He shivered.

"It looks like some sort of oil rig."

"Yeah, you're right. But I can't see if there's anyone on it. Maybe they have a telescope or something inside the lighthouse." They climbed into the large room which held the huge old light. The windows were broken, the fittings were rusted up and all the paint had peeled away from years of exposure.

"What about this?" Angus scratched inside an old cupboard and pulled out a pair of old binoculars.

"Brilliant." Jack took the binoculars and rested them on the frame of one of the broken panes. He pointed them in the direction of the wrecked rig.

"See anything?"

"It's definitely an oil rig. Completely messed up. Looks like there may have been a fire or something." Jack adjusted the focus. "Absolutely zero sign of life…"

Angus stood next to him, staring out in the same direction. "Hold on Jack! Bring them down a bit… look! There are footprints in the snow."

Jack lowered the glasses, "You're right! I can see them. Maybe Dad is out there. Maybe the Fenton guy has followed him or something. He could be in trouble. We need to go and check it out."

"I'm not sure, Jack, out there on the ice we'd be sitting ducks."

"But we can't just stand here and do nothing."

Angus grimaced. "OK – but let me at least get some kit from the stores so we don't freeze to death. Let's see if there's some outdoor clothing we can use."

Their climb down from the main lighthouse door to the ice below was not easy. From the castle on the mainland, the rock had looked precipitous and craggy, but that was nothing to what it was like close up. There were massive cliffs on all sides and the concrete walkway had crumbled away. With trepidation, Jack took a final step from the rock down onto the ice field. They had been right. There were clear footprints in the crust of snow that covered the ice.

Walking was not too difficult using the boots they had found in the stores, and they quickly reached the middle of the glinting ice field. It was not long before they arrived at the rig. Snow drifts had built up around the bottom of the rig and they could see where steps had been cut into the ice leading up onto the main platform. They peered up at the huge structure that loomed over them.

"What a beast!" Angus said.

Jack was still breathing hard from their hike across the ice. "I know rigs used to come into the Forth here for maintenance, but I've never seen one this size."

He craned his neck up to stare at the rig. "Look at that – the lettering – up there at the top of the accommodation block…" Angus followed Jack's eye-line. "Yes, I noticed on the way over. It's like a big sign… and it's got that funny logo… but I don't understand what it says; it looks like it's written in Chinese."

"I think you're right," Jack nodded. So how does a Chinese oil rig end up wrecked in the Firth of Forth in Scotland, forty years in the future and half a planet away from China… in a world that's turned to ice?"

Gingerly, they clambered up onto the metal surface of the platform and crept forward towards the middle of the giant rig. Jack found that using the railings was not much help because the metal was so cold his gloves would stick. After a few minutes of slipping and scrambling it became apparent that the structure was older and more precarious than they had first thought. The cold breeze that whipped around the old steel towers and cranes caused an eerie whistling sound.

"Look – the footprints go that way."

Jack pointed along a metal walkway which led to a block of dilapidated cabins built one on top of the other. The building was intact and seemed to have avoided the fire that had obviously torn through the rest of the structure.

They approached the door. It was metal and had an opening in its top half where there would have been a window – but the glass had long since fractured and gone. There was a sign on the wall next to the office that had been badly eroded.

"Some of this is in English," Jack said.

There was a string of lettering in Chinese, but underneath was an English translation, although it was hard to decipher.

Jack rubbed a finger over the sign, trying to read it. "Think I've got it:

HEAVENLY KINGDOM INDUSTRIES HYDROCARBON
GROUP – ARCTIC DIVISION
ARCTIC HORIZON PRODUCTION PLATFORM
– CONTROL CENTRE B

Beneath there were more words in a strange italic script:

"In the name of Christ."

Jack was bewildered.

"Heavenly Kingdom Industries? Doesn't sound like an evil global oil company," Angus said.

Jack was deep in concentration. "It says Arctic. Arctic division... but we're hundreds of miles from the North Pole. And how can it move around, if everything is iced up?"

"Maybe it came here for repairs or something and then all this ice came later? But is that possible? I mean, can an ice age happen that quickly... like just in a few years?"

"I don't know, but I've heard stuff about ocean currents pumping warm water up from the equator into the sea around Britain. I read once that with global warming, ice melts and dilutes the salt content of the sea, so the water from the equator stops pumping up our way. Then because there's no warm water, everything ends up freezing – it can tip the climate. Maybe that could cause a whole new ice age?"

Angus shrugged and pointed to the door of control centre, "You going to open it, then?"

Jack pulled open the door and then he screamed.

The body had been mummified with the cold. The lifeless eyes stared directly at Jack as he stood over the body in the doorway. Bizarrely the man was still wearing his blue overalls and sitting in his swivel chair in front of two computer terminals. But he looked like he had not moved for a very long time.

"That's gross," Angus said, turning away. "It's like the poor guy is still at work..."

Jack felt his stomach turn. "And as if he's staring at us."

Angus pushed the chair gently away. It was only a slight movement, but it was enough to disturb the position of the body in the chair, so it slipped, disintegrating as it fell face down on to the floor.

"Nice..."

They looked around the tops of the desks and in the drawers. Jack tried to keep his eyes away from the body.

"What about this?" Angus held up a dusty looking report, "The title – it's like the sign outside – half in Chinese but there's an English translation as well…"

"What does it say?"

"Health and Safety Inspection. Thirty-first of January 1976."

"But that's impossible," Jack said. "Look around… these computers – nothing like these existed then…. And the rig itself, all this technology, I'm sure it's too advanced… North Sea oil exploration didn't even start until the 1970s and I've never heard of anything going on in the Arctic."

"Weird. Hey – look at that?"

Angus nodded to a painting on the wall. It was completely out of place with the rest of the office – a crude black line drawing of a Chinese man. He wore a loose-fitting robe with a dragon on it and a strange-looking hat. Underneath the portrait were the words:

HONG XIUQUAN – BROTHER OF CHRIST AND FOUNDER OF THE HEAVENLY KINGDOM

"It's the same picture!" Jack exclaimed, "Remember? At the museum in Edinburgh, the woman giving the presentation about the Taiping Rebellion… she showed a picture… it's the same guy. I'm sure of it. He's the leader of the Taiping."

"Yeah – you're right. The Chinese seem to be following us around."

"Come on. I've had enough of this place and we still don't know what's happened to Dad. Let's head back to the rock, before it gets dark."

CHAPTER 9
- A CHINESE RIDDLE

B ack inside the lab, it was at least warm. They had raided the stores, managed to stoke up an ancient stove and the remains of a meal sat between them. Jack flicked through the report that they had retrieved from the rig and shook his head. "We're none the wiser," Angus said. "We know your dad and Fenton must have been here – but not what's happened to them. All we've got is an ancient, wrecked Chinese oil rig and a bunch of ice."

Jack nodded, "Maybe we need to make another search to see if we can find any more clues?" He looked at the array of terminals again. "But where do we start?"

The steady warmth from the stove and some food and drink were helping clear Jack's mind a little.

"All that ice up there... wouldn't just happen in forty years – it takes hundreds... thousands of years. And when Dad got here and discovered the whole world had ended in some icy hell... like us, he's must've asked why?" Jack rubbed his chin. "Question for us is, what did he do next?"

Suddenly, he had a brainwave.

"The Timeline Simulator! You know, the computer program they use to simulate how changes in history can affect the future. It must be accessed from one of these terminals. Dad might have used it to try and work out what happened in the past to cause the climate to flip."

Jack turned to the first terminal and started pounding away at the keyboard.

"Different icons… nothing here… maybe this one is better." Jack turned to another computer that was also on standby.

Angus moved behind Jack just as an application opened and the words – Timeline Simulator Version 7.3.1 – flashed onto the screen.

"Nice one."

Jack tapped the screen, "Saved simulations. And the last one – look! It was saved … two days ago. That must have been Dad! I'm going to run it."

They waited as the program opened. Jack leaned back. The screen showed a map of the world. In one corner there was a date counter. It started to count forward, and as is it did so, coloured shading on a map, showing the relative power of countries around the world, started to grow or recede.

Jack explained: "The counter starts at 1750 – so this scenario of Dad's starts then."

The small red blob showing Britain in the middle of the map slowly started to expand. As the counter cycled its way through the nineteenth century, the red shading across parts of the world spread like an infectious disease, enveloping India, Australia and Africa.

"I think that's showing the growth of the British Empire," Jack said.

The expansion of power of the other European nations was spreading too: blue for France and black for a unified Germany. The counter then moved on through the twentieth century to show the rise of the Soviet Union and the United States and the decline of the old European countries. As the counter reached and then passed the year 2000 another country started to grow in the East. Bar charts in the corner of the screen were changing rapidly, as that country began to overtake all others in population, wealth and military power.

"See – that must be the growth of China. It's taking off big time."

"It's stopped," Angus said. "Hold on, what's happening?"

A message popped up on the screen:

Baseline historical model completed. Stand by for start of updated historical model…

Then:

Updated historical timeline starting…

"It's back at 1750; it's starting again. This must be a new scenario that Dad modelled…"

Again, they saw the power of Britain and the other European countries start to grow, then something happened. In the Far East, in Southern China, in fact, a small black blob appeared that had not been on the map before. The blob started to get bigger. Jack looked at the date counter as it passed 1860.

Suddenly, the black blob enveloped the whole of China and then started to spread into Japan and other parts of the Far East.

"This is completely different from the first scenario – look at all the economic and military growth numbers. They're topping out at thirty-two per cent growth a year – that's really high, isn't it? It must mean that black blob which has taken over the whole of China is increasing its wealth and power incredibly quickly."

Suddenly the simulation stopped. The date stopped and winked back at them:

2048

"What does that mean?"

Jack looked down at the table. A notebook and pile of papers lay beside the terminal – he couldn't believe he hadn't noticed them before.

"Maybe there's something in this lot. Look someone's been scribbling here." He flicked through the pages until he reached one page with only a few words scrawled on it:

New historical timeline? Caused by…
intervention in the past?
Premature rise of China?
Competition for resources?
Point of Divergence = 1860?
Taiping rebels take Shanghai?
And finally:
2040s = end of civilisation?

The last sentence had three bold lines scrawled under it. "Look at this Angus… I reckon Dad wrote this. That's definitely his handwriting."

Angus shook his head. "End of civilisation, 2040s… that doesn't sound too clever… Hang on, that's now, we're in 2046 now!"

But Jack wasn't listening. He was deep in thought – it was like trying to assemble a complicated jigsaw puzzle in his head: the wrecked Chinese oil rig, the rise of China in the Timeline Simulator and his dad's notes.

"OK, this is what I think happened. Dad was at the Revisionist base and he wanted us to join him to show us something. But, before we arrived, he met this Fenton guy and maybe those two others and there was some sort of big bust up. The two men died, Dad got injured too and he used the Taurus to escape. He went to the future, and Fenton followed him. In the future he discovered something weird had happened. The climate had completely changed. At first he was shocked – like us – but then he started looking for clues. He went outside and saw the oil rig and he investigated. He discovered it was a Chinese oil rig – there was a picture of that Xiuquan guy from China in the 1850s, from the Taiping Rebellion, and that's really weird, because if I remember right from what I learned at the museum – the Taiping were defeated. But I think something has happened in the past to change that, and to make them victorious. Their victory would have led to other changes… they took over the whole of China and then pretty much the rest of Asia. You saw it in the simulation."

"And if China became a really powerful country – maybe they needed oil and that would explain how they came to be building big oil rigs for the Arctic in the 1970s," said Angus.

"Exactly. Dad ran the Timeline Simulator to see if it could tell him what had happened. His notes talk about an intervention in the past and a Point of Divergence in 1860 – that's the point in history when something happened to change the future – there was a split and somewhere along the line a different future started."

"So what caused the change in 1860? And how did it affect the climate so that everything turned to ice so quickly?"

"I have no idea. But Dad's note says the Taiping might have taken Shanghai, which is a big Chinese trading city and port. We have to find Dad… question is, where's he gone?" Worry lines creased Jack's forehead but suddenly his face lit up. "Of course, what an idiot I've been! We know exactly where he's gone!"

Angus followed Jack as he rushed back into the Taurus chamber. The great machine loomed over them as Jack examined the output from the control terminal.

"The online activity log…" Jack said. "It's all here…"

TAURUS ACTIVITY LOG
Departure summary:
Time Phone Serial: 002
Time Phone Holder: Tom C.
Departure Date: July 14th 2046 / 3:37 p.m.
Departure Location: Firth of Forth, Scotland.
Arrival summary:
Time Phone Serial: 002
Time Phone Holder: Tom C.
Arrival Date: August 20th 1860 / 9:35 a.m.
Arrival Location: Shanghai, Harbour Area, China.

Jack stabbed his finger at the screen, "There! China! Dad is in China! In fact, Shanghai – just as we thought."

"In the year 1860," Angus added.

"And look here – Fenton has followed him again!"

TAURUS ACTIVITY LOG
Departure summary:
Time Phone Serial: 009
Time Phone Holder: Fenton P.
Departure Date: July 15th 2046 / 4:40 p.m.
Departure Location: Firth of Forth, Scotland.
Arrival summary:
Time Phone Serial: 009
Time Phone Holder: Fenton P.
Arrival Date: August 18th 1860 / 9:07 a.m.
Arrival Location: Shanghai, Harbour Area, China.

"Fenton has followed Dad right back to China. But it looks like he arrived in Shanghai before Dad…"

"So he could spring a little surprise for your dad when he gets there. Says something about the harbour area."

"Yes. But this helps," Jack said hopefully. "We know Dad is in Shanghai, near the Harbour, in China in 1860. We know he's gone there because he's discovered that something has changed there in the past to alter the future. And it has to be something big – because it changed the climate and, well, it seems to have wiped every living thing off the earth. He's gone back to try and find out what's done that and to try and fix it."

"But in the meantime, this Fenton guy is right on his tail."

Jack looked at Angus, "I think it's pretty obvious what we do now, don't you?"

Angus's lip curled, "I've always fancied a trip East."

CHAPTER 10
– SHANGHAI SURPRISE

A shop. To be precise, a hardware shop. Jack first realised this when Angus – disorientated having been catapulted through the temporary wormhole – fell away from the landing spot and careered straight into a tall rack of wooden shelves. The shelving unit collapsed as Angus tumbled into it and there was a loud crash as boxes of nails, screws and washers sprayed everywhere. Angus groaned as he lay in a heap on top of the upended shelving with dust from the floor billowing all around.

Jack helped him on to his feet. "You OK?"

"I'll survive... where are we?"

Jack looked around anxiously. Their noisy arrival would cause consternation – in seconds they could be surrounded by irate customers and shop assistants. But as his eyes adjusted from the flash of light that signalled their arrival from the twenty-first century, he realised that the shop was strangely dark. In fact, the only light seemed to come from the cracks between a series of crude wooden planks nailed across the front windows. It was dusty and gloomy and fortunately there was no one home.

Jack had managed to grab a Revisionist undervest before they'd left – the time phone fit snuggly inside it. He pulled out the device from its pouch and flicked it open:

Date: August 17th, 1860
Time: 10:35 a.m.

Location: Shanghai, China.

His heart gave a little jump.

Angus dusted himself down, "What next? Fancy a Chinese?"

"Follow our plan. Try and blend in and make our way to the harbour area so we are ready to meet Dad when the activity log says he will arrive – in three days' time."

"We need to be on our guard though. Fenton arrives tomorrow."

"And he might not be too friendly."

Jack didn't hear what Angus said because, as he looked around, something on one of the shelves in the shop distracted him. For a moment he didn't take any notice, because it was such an everyday object. But as his eyes adjusted further to the gloom in the cluttered shop, he saw there was a whole row of them. He frowned.

"You coming, Jack? We don't want the shopkeeper to find we've trashed his store..."

"Angus?"

"What?"

"I'm looking at the time phone – and it says we're in 1860 right... I mean in Shanghai in 1860?"

"Right."

"Did they really have electric kettles then?" Jack nodded to the row of kettles on the shelf in front of them.

"Sorry?" Angus followed Jack's gaze. "Yeah – you're right. And look, over there... they've got... well they look like hair dryers."

Jack took a neat little torch from his slim backpack and started to flash it around the room. He spotted something on the wall near the shop doorway. A light switch. He flicked it on. There was an alarming crackling noise and then the whole shop was washed in a flickering, weak grey light. The full contents of the shop were unveiled before them – and it was an extraordinary sight. The shop was cluttered with all manner of ironmongery and hardware. But there were also electrical goods – kettles, lamps and heaters. They were electrical consumer goods – but their designs were not modern. They were crudely made and some had strange patterns and markings on them. Jack looked at Angus, who stood in the middle of the shop with a bemused expression on his face.

"Did they even have electricity... you know, in 1860?" Angus asked, mystified.

"Well, I think they did, er, do," Jack said. "But I'm pretty sure they didn't have electrification of whole cities – you know, to power shops like this one, or to power all the electrical goods in here. It's incredible. This sort of technology, well, it seems completely out of place – it's maybe seventy or eighty years ahead of its time..."

"There's other stuff over here," Angus said, "but I don't think these are electrical. Sewing machines, maybe? But these look like they're..." Angus peered closer, "Steam driven."

"And look at those weird things – pumps. This one looks like it's attached to a lawn mower engine or something..."

Angus placed his hand on the device, "I'd know one of these anywhere – it's a spark plug, and that's a carburettor and there's a little fuel tank there... it's a petrol engine."

"Well that makes no sense either – I'm sure these designs are too advanced for 1860."

"What do you think it means, Jack?"

"I don't know. It's weird... all these different technologies in one place – steam, electricity, petrol – it's like everything has been kind of mixed up together somehow... or," he bit his lip, "like technology is developing really quickly, so stuff like steam and petrol, have been discovered at the same time."

"What, or who, has triggered such a massive change?" Angus asked. "How did it happen?"

"I don't know," Jack shook his head. "Anyway, it makes no difference; we need to follow the same plan. Work our way across the city to the harbour to find Dad. Let's check the map on the app."

Jack reached into his undervest and pulled out his VIGIL device. Before their departure he had downloaded plenty of information from the Revisionist system about nineteenth-century China, including a rudimentary map of Shanghai.

"Here we go… first of all we need to try and work out where we are and then how we get to the harbour." Jack looked at Angus. "You ready for this?"

They unbolted the shop door and stepped out onto the street. It was humid and warm. In some ways it was what Jack imagined a Chinese city street to look like – flowing banners and signs in Chinese and a huge range of little shops and stalls.

But there was something Jack had not expected. The street was completely deserted. Just like the hardware shop where they had arrived. Everywhere was boarded up and there were no signs of life. Further along Jack noticed a makeshift barricade that had been erected across the street. There was no obvious way through it, and Jack had no idea why it was there. He walked further out into the street to get a better view of their new surroundings.

Suddenly, Angus screamed, "Jack, look out!"

CHAPTER 11
- TAIPING TERROR

Jack swung round. As if from nowhere a horseman was careering headlong down the street. He was heading straight for Jack, with a lance in his right hand. Jack could see he was about to be skewered, but he was frozen to the spot. Again, he heard Angus scream out his name… but it sounded oddly distant, as if he was underwater. Jack saw the horse's mouth foaming and the contorted face of the lancer as he let out a hideous battle cry, but he still couldn't move. Then, quite suddenly, the horseman lurched sideways and thrown from his saddle, landed awkwardly on the dusty road. The horse reared up, its forelegs kicking out centimetres from Jack's head, then it turned and cantered back up the street. Jack was still too stunned to move.

"Get back down here, if you want to live!" A voice shouted. Then Angus was beside him bundling him forward and he finally snapped out of his trance. A man dressed in a cavalry uniform with a red jacket and dark trousers was running towards them from the makeshift barricade further down the street. He had a huge handlebar moustache and wore a white pith helmet. Both the hat and uniform had seen better days. "Hurry!" he shouted.

As they ran for the barricade, Jack noticed the man's rifle. "Captain James Fleming. Dragoon Guards," the soldier thrust out a grubby hand. "Pleased to meet you, but how on earth do you come to be here? Haven't you heard? The whole Taiping rebel army is marching on Shanghai and the city is evacuating…"

The boys didn't have the breath to respond.

"Climb over that section there and get yourselves undercover, we're expecting the rest of this horde any minute… and I warn you – they're a hideous lot."

As they clambered over the barricade, they discovered that a number of troops had taken up position behind and actually inside it. Most wore uniforms similar to Captain Fleming's. There were British but also some Sikh soldiers from India, as well as one or two Chinese. Jack noticed two machine-gun posts built into the barricade. It was odd but, just like some of the things they had seen in the shop, the guns looked quite modern.

Captain Fleming was standing high up on the barricade. "Here they come!" he bellowed.

Looking through a gap in the barricade Jack could see that the Taiping cavalry charge had started. In seconds, the Taiping were racing straight at them in a maelstrom of thundering hooves, dust and metal.

"Hold your fire…" Fleming shouted, his voice steady, but a single shot rang out from a panicked soldier behind the barricade.

"Hold your damned fire!" Fleming raged.

Jack could see the eyes of the horsemen and feel the vibration of hooves through the ground. They were only a few metres away now. He closed his eyes and tried to dig himself deeper into the barricade.

"Fire!" Fleming boomed.

The whole place erupted. There was a cacophony of rifle and machine-gun fire; Jack thought his eardrums might burst.

"Cease fire!" Fleming bellowed.

The gunfire stopped and Jack looked out onto the street. The Taiping cavalry charge had been halted in its tracks and all that was left was a mass of dead and dying men and horses lying in the dust. "Jones, Sutcliffe – get out there and finish 'em off. Rest of you – reload – there're more… don't you worry about that. These Taiping – there's no end to the blighters."

Fleming jumped down from his position on top of the barricade.

"Sorry about that gentlemen… looks like you've got yourself caught up in the middle of a pitched battle. 'Fraid we're not going to be able to hold out here much longer. We'll have to retreat back to the main defence line." Fleming looked at them with a beady eye as he reloaded his pistol. "Anyway, what's your story?"

"We got separated from our family, er, our father is a… trader… er… we're heading to the waterfront." Jack tried to sound convincing.

"You're from the British concession? Well, you're in the wrong part of town. It's lucky you bumped into us. We've got ammunition to fight off one more attack and then we need to regroup. I'll give it two or three more days before Shanghai is completely overrun. The Taiping rebels have got limitless men, it seems…. and they're well-armed… got some modern weapons too… though sometimes they like to do things the old-fashioned way," he cast his eye out on to the street at the heaped corpses of men and horses. "Such a waste, but I'm not complaining – it's us or them."

The captain was interrupted by one of his men, yelling down from the top of the barricade. "Cap'n – they're coming again – even more!"

"Gawd. Already?" Captain Fleming's face was set in grim determination. "They're gluttons for punishment, this lot. Fanatics. You gents keep down here. We'll fight then off and then we'll be retreating… we'll get you to safety, don't worry about that."

But as Fleming stepped back to the barricade, a violent explosion came from behind them, and a powerful shockwave hit them like an express train. Jack was propelled backwards and landed awkwardly amid a cloud of dust. He spluttered and raised his head, peering through the swirling dust. The line of shops on the opposite side of the street had completely collapsed. They were now just a smoking heap of bricks and masonry. Jack pulled himself to his feet, dazed and shaken, but OK. Then he spotted Angus lying on the road next to him. He had caught the full force of the blast and his face was white with dust and plaster. Blood was oozing from a wound on his forehead, but he looked like he was still breathing – just. There were people rushing around, shouting and pointing, but all Jack could hear was the deafening ringing in his ears. He bent down to help Angus, but out of the corner of his eye, he noticed a huge dark shape lurching towards them, over the rubble created by the collapsed shops. It crawled forward and then stopped.

Jack couldn't believe what he was seeing; it was an absolute monster. A battle tank, the usual caterpillar tracks, turret and main gun – yet unlike any tank Jack had ever seen. It was painted with an extraordinary black and red livery and had Chinese writing scrawled all over its sides. Two enormous flags billowed from the turret. Suddenly, a forward machine gun on the tank opened up and bullets ripped into the rear of the barricade. Then the muzzle of the tank's massive main gun flashed and a shell buried itself in the barricade, which erupted in a storm of flying splinters and shards. At the same time the Taiping tank had attacked through the rear of the barricade, a second head-on cavalry charge was co-ordinated to the front. It took Fleming and his men completely by surprise. Jack watched in horror as the Taiping warriors began clambering over the barricade. The defenders were powerless to stop them, and Fleming's attempt at an orderly retreat quickly turned into a rout. The soldiers were fleeing down the street away from the wrecked barricade. Jack grabbed Angus's arm and urged him to his feet. Angus groaned.

"My head…"

"It's just a scratch, come on, we need to get out of here…" But Jack was too late. A swarthy arm encircled his midriff and he felt himself lifted from the ground. He was then plonked a few metres away and forced onto his knees. Jack looked up at his assailant – a huge Chinese Taiping warrior. The warrior nodded over at Captain Fleming and several of the soldiers who had also been captured by the marauders. Like Jack, they were kneeling, and they were banging their heads on the ground – kowtowing. Jack looked back up at the warrior, not quite understanding what they were doing and why. The warrior jammed the butt of his sword into Jack's ribcage. It was excruciatingly painful. The warrior grasped Jack's hair and banged his head into the ground repeatedly. Just like the action of Fleming and the other soldiers, it seemed Jack was to keep banging his head into the ground until someone told him to stop. The warrior moved to do the same to Angus, who was still a little dazed and confused from the explosion.

The Taiping rebels now had full control of the barricade and the tank was starting to rip it apart to open up the street. Soon there was a pathway through for the horses and a posse set off in pursuit of the fleeing defenders. Jack, Angus, Fleming and the other captives were hauled up from the ground and pushed roughly into a line across the street. They were surrounded by Taiping warriors, but there was one who was clearly in charge. He was shouting something in Mandarin. Jack suddenly felt his hands wrenched behind his back and tied by a cord. Ahead, a Taiping cavalryman dismounted and approached – he was even larger than Jack's assailant. He held an enormous broad-bladed cleaver loosely in one hand. He walked round the back of the soldier next to Jack as the officer issued another command. From the corner of his eye, Jack saw the cavalryman grasp his neighbour by the hair and push him forward. The cleaver glinted momentarily in the sunlight and then wheeled downwards onto the man's exposed neck. The head rolled away from the body. Jack retched with horror at the sight, but then he felt a hand grasp his own hair.

He was next.

CHAPTER 12
- JOSIAH

At first Jack didn't hear the distant cough and splutter of a rather old, badly made engine. His eyes were shut tight as he waited helplessly for the cold steel to slice through his neck. At least it would be quick, he thought. But nothing happened. In fact, the street was strangely silent after the onslaught of the Taiping attack – except for one thing. The noise of the engine was getting closer. Jack dared to open one eye and then look up. A strange-looking vehicle – like an open-topped vintage car – puttered to a halt just beyond the remains of the barricade. The throng of Taiping warriors stood to attention as a portly gentleman clambered down from the jalopy and bustled towards them. He had wisps of grey hair that covered a balding head and his fat, round face was very red. He looked completely out of place in the dusty Shanghai street where the Chinese Taiping cavalry had just fought a bloody engagement with the British King's Royal Dragoons. He scurried through the hole in the barricade to where Jack, Angus, Captain Fleming and the other captives were still lined up. The strange new arrival looked just like an English country vicar. He wore simple black robes and a white dog collar. As he bustled towards them, Jack felt the rough hands that held him slowly ease their grip.

The vicar went straight up to the Taiping officer and bellowed directly into his face. If Jack had not been so terrified, it would have seemed funny: a portly English vicar, completely unarmed, dressing down a great Taiping warrior about twice his height, who wore great swathes of leather and chain armour and had a deadly sword in his belt and a rifle strapped to his back. The warrior bowed his head in shame and the other men looked at their feet nervously as the vicar railed at them. He stopped shouting and scurried over to Jack, Angus and Captain Fleming. Jack felt himself hauled to his feet and with the deft slice of a knife his hands were released from their bonds. The others were similarly released, and Jack risked a glance at Angus. His friend winked back, and Jack sighed inwardly with relief that, for the moment, they were both in one piece.

"Gentlemen, gentlemen, I am so dreadfully sorry, a most terrible misunderstanding..." The vicar clicked his fingers and issued an order in Mandarin. Immediately bowls of water were proffered to the captives. Jack sucked his down gratefully. His heart was still racing, but the water tasted good and he sensed a dawning elation from his narrow escape.

"I'm afraid they do get carried away sometimes..." the vicar continued.

Fleming thrust out a hand. "Captain Fleming, Royal Dragoons... thank you for saving us, sir, and who might you be?"

"Delighted, Captain," the vicar twittered, "my name is Backhouse. Reverend Josiah Backhouse. I am, er, special advisor to General Li Xiucheng of the Taiping army... and," Backhouse added apologetically, "I'm afraid, gentlemen, that you will have to come with us."

The captain's whiskers twitched. "Sir, may I remind you that I am a captain in the Royal Dragoons. You shall release us now!"

The vicar looked embarrassed by Fleming's brave outburst and he peered at his feet. "I'm sorry, Captain, but that will simply not be possible. I'm afraid you are now prisoners of war," he turned to Jack and Angus, "all of you."

"You are aware, sir," Fleming continued, "that there is a major British force in Shanghai evacuating our civilians from the British Concession, and there are seventeen thousand British and French troops under James Hope Grant sailing north together to confront the Imperial emperor, as we speak? Once they have dealt with him,

I have no doubt they can come and deal with you and your Taiping rebel friends. Her Majesty's government does not take the kidnapping of its subjects lightly... whether by Chinese Taiping rebels or Chinese Imperialists."

"Quite so, quite so, Captain," the vicar waved his hand dismissively. "I am aware of the diplomatic situation, but I am afraid that you are now in my care..." He gestured at the Taiping cavalry around them. "I certainly don't want to hand you over to our friends here... they can be a little unpredictable..." He looked over at the detached head that rested in the street – some distance from its body. "As you have already witnessed."

Jack, Angus and the captain were marched to the vicar's strange vintage car and they clambered into some cramped seats in the back as their fellow captives stared after them bemused.

"Don't worry," Backhouse assured them. "Your companions will not be harmed."

He poked the driver, and the car's rough engine burst into life. "We're still perfecting the design, but I hope you find it comfortable, gentlemen." They rumbled their way back down the street, escorted by a contingent of the Taiping horsemen. As the car trundled on, all Jack could think about was what chance they would have of intercepting his father when he arrived in three days. It wasn't looking good.

"Where are you taking us?" the captain pressed.

"Please, Captain Fleming, we will be there soon enough." Josiah turned back to them from the front passenger seat, dabbing the sweat on his podgy face with a handkerchief, "First you must introduce me to your young friends." He looked at Jack and then at Angus, his eyes lingering on Jack who returned the stare uneasily.

"I say young man, don't I recognise you from somewhere?"

"I don't think so – I've never seen you before." Jack thought fast. "Er, we have spent most of our lives outside England."

This seemed to satisfy Backhouse who turned away with a shrug. Jack, however, thought it really odd that this strange-looking country vicar, completely out of place in the dust and heat of a Shanghai street in late summer, might somehow think they had met before.

"How did you two come to find yourselves manning a barricade in a city under siege?" Josiah asked.

"Our father... he's a trader," Jack lied. "We got lost in the confusion... the captain here saved our lives... we got split up during your attack. My father is expecting to meet us at the waterfront... we need to go back. You need to let us go."

"I am very sorry to hear about that. But there is no chance I can release you."

"These young men must be reunited with their family, Backhouse..." the captain began.

"We're not reuniting anyone for the moment. The city will still be very dangerous but I promise that all of you will be returned in due course." Backhouse said brightly. Then his tone changed and he muttered under his breath, "Assuming we get co-operation from the British government."

This was too much for the captain. "You call yourself a man of God, Backhouse, yet here you are in league with these Taiping barbarians," he burst out.

Josiah's red face turned a little redder. "Captain, your comments are uninformed – like those of so many of our English countrymen. The Taiping are hardly barbarians. They are our Christian brothers, fighting a holy and just civil war against the corrupt and decadent Imperialist Qing dynasty."

But as Jack peered from the back of the strange car which lumbered its way through the outskirts of Shanghai, he did not see much that could be described as holy or just. Everywhere he looked there was devastation from the Taiping assault on the city. Smoke plumes rose from burned-out huts and houses, and at points along the road bodies were piled up high. Taiping were everywhere – squads of infantry marching at the double into Shanghai, cavalry patrolling the streets, and, occasionally, armed wagons.

"Look at all this," Fleming said, "the misery of war... and all aided by you Backhouse – a supposed Christian. At home in London, they say you are a traitor."

"Thank you for your opinions," Backhouse said, his voice sounding strained, for the first time. "I would ask, simply, that you to keep them to yourself if you want to retain my co-operation; but just so you know, the hypocrisy of my English brethren never fails to astonish me..."

The captain fell silent.

After an hour or so, they crested a low rise in the road. Jack's head had nodded onto Angus's shoulder, but now Angus nudged him. The sight before them made Jack's jaw drop. Stretching for miles into the hazy distance were tents and bivouacs, set out in orderly rows, swarming with Taiping troops in red coats and conical white straw hats. They had reached the Taiping army encampment outside Shanghai. As they drew close, Jack started to distinguish between different parts of the camp. Alongside the cavalry and infantry was an enclosure of parked up tanks – each one just like the monster that had surprised them back at the barricade. Next to this, there was an encampment of artillery – though the guns were unlike any Jack had seen before. They were painted with slogans and emblazoned with all manner of extravagant decorations and motifs. Along the central axis of the camp, was the most extraordinary sight of all. A series of monster steam engines parked up one next to the other. Jack had seen pictures of old-fashioned steam engines once used for road works and on farms – and these machines were similar. They were great iron and bronze contraptions which belched black smoke and steam. Some had massive bulldozer attachments on the front and others had fortified turrets, with evil-looking guns sticking out of them. Jack remembered the little Shanghai hardware shop where he and Angus had seen different technologies somehow co-existing – it was the same here, in the Taiping army camp. The uniforms, flags and regalia could have been medieval, as were the lances and great cleavers that the infantry and cavalry carried. But other used technologies much more modern – steam-powered engines and crude petrol-driven machines, artillery and firearms that looked as if they belonged in a more modern age. Everything was mixed up.

Angus was mesmerised by the range of weaponry, but Jack caught Backhouse's eye as he surveyed the scene. He had a look of pride on his face.

"I will admit my Taiping friends have got some strange ideas, on both Christian doctrine and on government," he said. "But you can't fault their energy and organisation. And this army…" He turned to the captain and said, "The British government would be quaking in its boots if they could see it."

Fleming grunted.

"We are nearly there." Backhouse said something to the driver and pointed. "You will be taken to a holding tent – normal procedure – there will be refreshments, so please try and make yourselves comfortable. I will come back for you shortly."

With this, Backhouse stepped down from the jalopy and scurried off. Jack, Angus and Fleming were escorted to a nearby marquee which was enclosed in a wooden stockade.

"Prison," the captain said matter-of-factly.

But once inside the tent, they were offered tea and food; there was even water to wash themselves.

"You have heard of him, captain?" asked Jack. "I mean Backhouse – you seemed to know of him. You said he was known in England as a traitor?"

"You haven't heard of Josiah Backhouse? Where have you been my lad? Yes, he's famous; infamous more like. And he's a traitor indeed. I couldn't believe it was him."

"We are away most of the time… with our father," Angus chipped in, pleased with himself for having picked up on Jack's story.

"Well, Backhouse is a British missionary... but he's more than that, much more," the captain sipped his tea from a bowl. "Not quite how my mother makes it... but I have to say that tastes good." He looked around at the inside of the tent and groaned with frustration, "Can't believe I've got myself captured..."

"What do you mean, he's a traitor?" Jack tried to bring Fleming back to Backhouse.

"Aye, well... Backhouse was high up in the CPS... you know with all the Science Lords."

"CPS?"

The Captain looked at Jack oddly. "You really have missed out on your education, haven't you, my lad? CPS stands for 'Cambridge Philosophical Society' – they are a very powerful group of men. They advise the British government." He put a hand up to his mouth and whispered conspiratorially, "Some say they pretty much are the British government..."

"Oh?"

"Charles Babbage is the President of the CPS – has been for thirty years." The captain saw the confused look on Jack's face. "Now don't tell me you've never heard of Babbage? Inventor of the Difference Engine, the internal combustion engine, harnessing electrical energy, new weapons for the army and navy and of course, manned flight..."

"What? You've got planes as well?" Angus blurted out, then held a guilty hand to his mouth, which failed to disguise his astonishment.

The captain frowned, "You two... I mean, have you never been in the real world?"

"It's complicated..." Angus said.

Jack frowned and tried to move the captain on, "The CPS – are they the source of all these inventions – the weapons, steam engines, cars, electricity...? When, er, when did it start, I mean, when did they start inventing all these things?"

The captain's brow furrowed. "It started when I was a nipper. Now my father always used to say that in the old days Babbage was considered a bit of a joke – an eccentric. Ordinary folk didn't like him much, but then, in the 1830s all that changed. He, and his fellow scientists in the CPS, started to produce inventions, designs, machines... the most incredible scientific advances... they changed the world. It all started at the Trinity Conference..."

"What was that?" blurted Angus.

"Oh, it was a very significant event. March 31st 1836, in the Wren Library at Trinity College in Cambridge. It was the first CPS conference, when Babbage first announced some of the most amazing inventions that the CPS had created. All the top brass was there – it took the world by storm."

"Do you remember it?" said Jack.

"Yes – well I'm too young to remember it – but my father talks about it to this day and about the rumours that started circulating soon after. Some people thought the inventions were magic... or witchcraft even. All I can say is had Babbage and the other members of the CPS been anything other than British – it would have been the end of the British Empire and probably the end of us, because the scientific and military advances were profound."

"So where does Josiah Backhouse fit in?"

"An interesting story. Backhouse was in the CPS, close to Babbage, some say he was his right-hand man. I believe he was actually at the Trinity Conference. But then something happened. He was a Christian – nothing wrong with that of course – but he was fanatical." The captain tapped his temple with a finger. "Not all there, they say. Anyway, when he heard about this Taiping Rebellion, here in China, and that they were fellow Christians fighting a civil war against the corrupt Imperial dynasty, he decided he would make it his mission to help them. Didn't know he was here in Shanghai, mind you."

"They accepted him, then?" Jack interrupted. "The Taiping rebels, I mean?"

"There are a few supporters of the Taiping in Europe and England... missionaries, Christians. And Backhouse had something to offer the Taiping."

"What was that?" Angus said.

"He was close to Babbage, so he knew all about these incredible CPS inventions and how they were starting to make use of them as machines... and weapons. He started passing some of the secrets of these discoveries to the Taiping. At first the CPS and the British government had no idea. No one at home took much notice of the Taiping Rebellion, a civil war in China, on the other side of the world didn't really affect us. Of course, you're traders, so you know that mostly the British are interested in the trade – and all that's done through the ports – Hong Kong, Shanghai and the like where there are the European concessions. Meanwhile there was a civil war raging in the south of China between the Taiping and the Imperialist Qing. Then we started to hear strange things about British-designed arms turning up in China. At first we thought it was gun-running. War attracts all sorts of low-life – people who are happy to make a bit of money out of other people's misery. Then we heard new stories. That these Taiping rebels were starting to build whole factories in the south of China where they ruled. Soon we discovered that the Taiping were starting to build their own versions of CPS inventions. No one understood how they could have got hold of the designs. Then one day a trader said that he had seen an English missionary in Canton who seemed to be friendly with some of the Taiping leaders. Investigations were made – and what do you know? The missionary, it turned out, was our friend Backhouse. Next thing, he had disappeared into the Chinese interior and joined up with the Taiping for good. Now he's one of their leading chaps... you saw how those warriors obeyed him."

"He sounds bonkers. What does he want with us?" Angus said.

The captain shrugged. "I can make a guess – he wants to use us as bargaining chips..."

"How do you mean?" asked Jack. "Who would he be bargaining with?"

"With the British, of course. We're the most powerful country in the world and trade with China is important. To be honest, we don't really care who's in charge in China – whether it is the Imperialists or the Taiping rebels – as long as we can trade and make money. I reckon if the Taiping have three British hostages – including an army captain – it's one way that Backhouse and the Taiping can put pressure on the British to support them against the Imperialists. In fact, the British and French are virtually at war with the Imperialists already. Those seventeen thousand troops are marching on Beijing because they say the Imperialists have broken their last treaty, which was to open up more Chinese ports for trade."

Jack's brow furrowed as he tried to take it all in. "So, you've got a civil war going on in China between the Taiping in the south and the Imperialist Qing in the north. The British and French have got trading concessions in ports up and down the coast and they've sent an army to force the Imperialists in Beijing to open up trade even more. And now, here in Shanghai, the British are also trying to help defend an Imperial city from the Taiping who are trying to take it over?"

"That's about it," Fleming said. "The Taiping want Shanghai because it is a major sea port. It's just unfortunate that there are lots of Europeans there already."

"What a mess," Angus shook his head.

"Yes – and it doesn't help our cause with turncoats like Backhouse around – whether he's a Christian or not."

Suddenly, the door to the tent opened and Backhouse appeared, flanked by two burly Taiping guards.

"I think it is time, gentlemen – are you suitably refreshed?" But Backhouse did not wait for an answer. "Good, good. Now, you will be excited to hear that we have an audience with General Li Xiucheng himself. He is a fine man and he has a few questions. Excuse the indignity, but I am afraid you will have to be searched.

We have to be careful – hidden weapons that sort of thing – usual procedure."

Suddenly the Taiping guards stepped forward and Jack felt his clothes being ripped off him.

"Hey – get off !"

Backhouse shouted in Mandarin and the guards eased off. "I can do it myself, OK?"

But Jack's shirt and his undervest had been ripped in the clumsy assault, and as he pulled off the vest, something clattered to the floor. Jack stared down in horror. It was his VIGIL smart device.

Backhouse spotted it on the wooden floor and immediately bent down to pick it up.

Jack made a grab for it and shouted, "No! It's mine!"

The guards were too quick. They secured Jack in a vicelike grip. Angus started to move, but before he could take a step he too was immobilised.

Backhouse cradled the smooth plastic and metal device in his hand, inspecting it from every angle, and his expression slowly changed from one of bemusement to one of wonder.

"Extraordinary…" he whispered. He stared at the device and then back at Jack who was still held back by the guards, "Utterly extraordinary… just as I remember it… the 'Seeing Engine'… the Babbage 'Seeing Engine'."

Backhouse's dark, piggy eyes trained on Jack. "My young friend… where on God's earth did you get this?"

Jack was struggling to find any words. "I…"

"Leave him alone!" Angus shouted out suddenly. But he was quickly silenced by a loud slap across the face.

"Silence!" Backhouse bellowed, his face now purple. But, embarrassed by this sudden outburst, quickly he tried to collect himself.

"Now, if I remember, you press this, and…" Backhouse's face lit up, "yes, it comes alive! Just like the Engine… it is the same… a miracle!" He looked up at the ceiling. "Thank you, Lord." He stared at Jack and said menacingly, "You will explain to us how you come to be in possession of the Babbage 'Seeing Engine' and how you come to be in Shanghai. We will go to General Li Xiucheng now and show him our discovery."

The three of them were escorted to a cluster of tents at the centre of the encampment. The biggest marquee was guarded by two armour-clad Taiping riflemen in fur caps. Two golden lion flags flapped in a gentle breeze next to the entrance and ribbons fluttered from the eaves of the marquee. Stepping inside was like being transported to a different world. The walls and ceiling of the marquee were made of yellow silk and there was an elaborately woven carpet on the floor. Jack's eye was drawn to desk and chairs, intricately carved in red lacquer. Two clerks sat at separate desks and two more guards stood, blank-faced, at the back of the room. A Chinese man, in his thirties and wearing a bright red silk jacket, appeared from behind a curtain. This was General Li Xiucheng – commander of the great Taiping army. He gestured for Backhouse, Jack, Angus and Fleming to sit in chairs in front of his desk. A girl entered the tent and poured tea into the cups that stood on the desk in front of them. She bowed, moved aside and hovered, waiting for further orders.

Backhouse was bursting with excitement as he clutched the device.

"If I may, General?"

Xiucheng nodded and Backhouse approached the desk and tentatively laid the VIGIL device on the table in front of him. Amongst the splendour of the silk tent and the elaborate lacquer furniture, the device looked strangely out of place.

General Xiucheng raised his eyebrows at Backhouse, "What is this, Holy Teacher?"

"General, this is an extraordinary discovery. We have been blessed. It is a gift from God."

There was scarcely any change in the expression on Xiucheng's face.

"Explain, Holy Teacher," he commanded.

"This object was with these English hostages we picked up as we entered Shanghai. Only one of these devices has ever been seen before. It was invented by Charles Babbage in England. Babbage – the President of the Cambridge Philosophical Society, the leader of the Science Lords and Lucasian Professor of Mathematics. This device is so powerful that only three people ever knew of its existence... I was one of those people. Babbage guarded its secrets very, very carefully. But now we have the device, or a copy of it, delivered right into our hands. It is incredible."

"What does it... do?" Xiucheng said, calmly, staring at the strange gadget lying on the desk in front of him.

"No, it's not what it does, General, but what it shows. Let me demonstrate."

Backhouse switched on the device, opened one of the applications and started to scroll through a series of images. As he did so, Xiucheng's neutral expression changed to one of utter astonishment.

"Babbage never explained how he came to invent such a thing or how he created the pictures and designs that it shows. All we know is that it describes in detail some wondrous inventions and machines... machines that can be built. This, General, is the ultimate source of British power. The CPS inventions that drive British industry and military might come from this little box – the Babbage 'Seeing Engine' – and now it has been delivered straight into our hands." Backhouse was finding it difficult to control himself, "I felt, when Babbage showed me what he had created, all those years ago, it was as if he had received a gift from the almighty... a window to a different world. Today God has given us, the Taiping, that same gift. It is a message that God is with us. The information in the 'Seeing Engine' will allow us to build even more powerful machines... and weapons... weapons you could imagine in your wildest dreams. General, the Taiping will rule the earth – the whole world will become the Heavenly Kingdom. Our Heavenly Kingdom."

Jack observed the exchange between Backhouse and General Xiucheng. It was like watching a slow-motion car crash. It was a disaster. It would bring a torrent of unwelcome questions. Jack knew he would be expected to reveal its secrets and help translate them into real, working machines – machines that would be used to help the Taiping win their civil war against the Imperialists. The Taiping had already benefited from industrial and military secrets seeping into the country, but the discovery of their own VIGIL device would give them access to new ideas and innovations which would accelerate this process and quickly translate into a huge military advantage. He felt ill.

General Xiucheng was now nodding slowly at Backhouse. "We must go to Nanjing," he said. "It will be safer and we need to discuss the implications of this with Hong Rengan and the Heavenly King himself. We must make arrangements immediately. There is no time to lose."

"What's he talking about?" Angus whispered to Fleming.

"Nanjing – it is the Taiping capital city – up river," the captain replied out of the corner of his mouth."

As they were escorted from General Xiucheng's tent, Jack noticed the young servant girl who had brought in the tea earlier. She stood stock still at the entrance to the tent, her head bowed in respect. But for some reason, as Jack passed her, she raised her face to his. It was the briefest and most subtle of movements and Jack nearly missed it. She was very pretty and for an instant Jack could not help looking her straight in the eye. Then, for a reason Jack could not begin to fathom, she smiled at him.

CHAPTER 13
– INTO THE HEAVENLY KINGDOM

The journey on the Yangtze river to Nanjing took two hot, sticky and uncomfortable days. General Xiucheng entered the city in triumph. He could announce the capture of the port of Shanghai to his leader, the Heavenly King, in person. But there was an added bonus – the capture of a British army officer and the momentous discovery of the mysterious Babbage 'Seeing Engine' and two interpreters of its fantastic secrets: Jack and Angus. General Xiucheng, wearing flowing gold robes and a jewelled crown, was carried in a special chair. Backhouse, Jack and Angus rode some way behind, ringed by an escort of fierce-looking Taiping guards. Captain Fleming was not with them. There were still occasional raids on the river by the Imperialists from the north against the Taiping rebels and General Xiucheng thought it best to split up the hostages.

Ahead, Jack could see the huge walls – twenty metres high – that enclosed the city of Nanjing in a vast triangle. The gate they entered into to the city led through a ten-metre long tunnel that burrowed through the massive walls.

"Behold!" Backhouse announced. "The Kingdom of Heaven." But as far as Jack could see, it looked nothing like the Kingdom of Heaven. He was shocked at the squalor – children played in the filthy streets and there were scores of beggars. "We are rebuilding, of course. There is no money and no one owns property. The state provides everything. In this way, people are free to work and to follow the teachings of the Heavenly King. No more corruption, no more greed, no more Imperialism…"

Periodically, military drum and gong signals boomed across the city from lookout towers high up on the walls.

"They've got enough soldiers," Angus said, gaping at the scene before them.

"Ah, the military – the heart of the Taiping." Backhouse waxed, "The Imperialists, by contrast, are cowardly, ill-disciplined and corrupt. Mind you, they are starting to get better. Despite our efforts, the new technologies are starting to seep in… I hear they have airships now, and they have many spies who have stolen secrets from us… you would be surprised. They will even have spies here – in Nanjing. But very soon we will have completely overrun Shanghai and we will have a sea port and, of course, a genuine Babbage 'Seeing Engine' There will be no stopping the Taiping," Backhouse announced triumphantly. "Today China – tomorrow, the world!" Angus and Jack exchanged glances.

They rounded a corner and the city changed. The street broadened out and well-kept gardens appeared on either side. There was extensive building work underway and rickety bamboo scaffolding clung to emerging yellow-walled buildings. "There!" Backhouse waved. "The Palace of the Heavenly King. Isn't it magnificent?"

The building took Jack's breath away. An enormous half-built palace rose into the sky – all towers and upward-pointing eaves in the Chinese style. Vast silk drapes and flags hung from the walls, adorned with Chinese writing, symbols and dragons.

The procession came to a halt and a small detachment escorted General Xiucheng through an imposing front gate. Jack, Angus and Backhouse followed in a further group at a respectable distance. They walked through a series of courtyards and rock gardens adorned with miniature trees, hedges and sculptures, until they arrived at a vast pavilion decorated with paintings, gilded flags and lanterns. It was furnished with a desk, a table and chairs – all in the same beautifully carved red lacquer work that Jack had first seen in General Xiucheng's tent at the encampment outside Shanghai. They waited for a while until a rather plump little man appeared from behind a curtain and scurried in.

"His Excellency Hong Rengan, First Minister of the Heavenly Kingdom," Backhouse announced.

Rengan greeted General Xiucheng in Mandarin. He eyed Jack and Angus and then, to their surprise, addressed Backhouse in flawless English.

"We received your messages. You have it then? This discovery... this 'engine'?"

Backhouse flashed a look at General Xiucheng and then fished out the VIGIL device from under his frock coat. Rengan's eyes bulged in wonder as Backhouse tapped on the screen and scrolled through some of the images.

"If what you say is true, total victory for the Taiping is assured. This calls for celebration." He clapped his hands and barked an order. "Now..." he turned to Jack and Angus and put a fatherly arm around their shoulders. "You two have been on a long journey. You are far from Shanghai and far from home, hungry and tired. We will eat and we will drink and then you will rest. When we are all ready, you will show us the secrets of the 'Seeing Engine'."

Jack and Angus were led away from the pavilion to an annex across the courtyard. It was luxuriously appointed, except that there were no windows and the door was locked behind them. Jack sat on a low bed and put his head in his hands.

"This is a nightmare."

"Tell me about it. But what I don't get is that Backhouse recognised your VIGIL device. He must have seen one before. He said that this Babbage guy had one exactly the same back in England... but how can that be?"

Jack looked up. "Incredible isn't it? I've been trying to work it out... Want to know what I think?"

"We've got all day." Angus gave a crooked smile.

"OK. I think Babbage somehow got hold of a VIGIL device like our one and studied it meticulously. That's what helped him and the Cambridge Philosophical Society create all these new inventions we're seeing which shouldn't exist in 1860. The conference that Fleming mentioned was twenty-five years ago, so the inventions have had time to develop and they've seeped from Britain across the rest of the world, including to Backhouse's Taiping friends right here."

Angus nodded. "Right, I can understand that – Babbage must have got hold of the device years ago – but how did he get it in the first place?"

Jack shook his head slowly, "That's what we need to find out. I can only think of one way it could have happened. A VIGIL agent must have travelled back in time and given it to him."

"But why? VIGIL would never do that. It's against all the rules."

Jack nodded in agreement. "I know, Angus, I know. But how else could it have happened?"

"You've heard of this Babbage guy before?"

"Yeah. He's famous. He was a genius. In 'real' history he invented computers about a hundred years before anyone else. He called them 'Engines' – there was a 'Difference Engine' and an 'Analytical Engine' – basically they were calculating computers but with metal cogs and levers and dials and stuff. I can imagine that if someone that brilliant was given a VIGIL device he could easily use it to make up some of the designs it shows. There's some pretty detailed stuff in some of those apps."

Angus nodded.

"There's something else I've been thinking about..."

Angus raised his eyebrows, "What?"

"It's two days since we left Shanghai... remember what the Taurus log said...?"

"You mean – your Dad?"

"Right. He'll be in Shanghai shortly and we'll be stuck here in this festering pit more than two days away…"

"And Fenton must be here already…" Angus grimaced.

"Yes, waiting for Dad. But there's one thing we need to remember…" Jack reached into his torn undervest to the special pocket. He pulled out the time phone.

Jack smiled. "They were so excited at finding the VIGIL device that they forgot to search the rest of me. Whilst we've still got a time phone, we've still got hope."

Angus grinned. "Of course… no signal I guess?" They peered at the time phone.

"Stupid thing is always dead when you need it most. We just need to be patient."

"When we get a signal, we can time travel and be ready to meet your Dad when he gets to Shanghai."

"We just have to keep ourselves out of trouble until then."

"Can't see that being a problem." Angus smiled. "Way I see it, Backhouse and his Taiping cronies need to look after us – they think we're the ones that can help them use the VIGIL device." He nodded at the time phone, "You better put that somewhere very safe – you don't want them to get hold of that as well – then there'd be total carnage."

There was a rattle at the door. Backhouse, Rengan and two burly guards entered the room. The guards handed each boy silk robes to put on and then they were led away from the pavilion and back through the palace. They crossed a courtyard – fringed with miniature trees that sprang from ornate flower beds. Ahead, Jack could see a great archway.

"The Inner Temple. Usually only women attend the Heavenly King in the Inner Palace. You are privileged indeed," Backhouse said with an excited smile.

"Where are we going?" Jack asked.

"We have an audience with the Heavenly King, the leader of the Taiping. You bow and you say nothing, of course. You will be in the presence of the divine. The brother of Jesus Christ, he is not of this earth." Backhouse said the words with a quiet intensity. Jack gave Angus a sidelong glance. Jack had seen and experienced many extraordinary things over the last few months, but the idea that they were about to meet the brother of Christ stretched the bounds of reason. It was becoming increasingly clear to Jack that Josiah Backhouse was completely unhinged.

They were left to wait for some time in an anteroom, where there was a heavy smell of incense. By the time they were summoned again, both boys ached with tiredness, but on entering the chamber their eyes widened in amazement. The room was brightly decorated in gold and red silk and lit by flickering lanterns. Ahead, was a bed upon which reclined a figure in magnificent white and gold robes. In the shadows, Jack discerned several figures – all women – dressed in silk robes and wearing high head-dresses. One of the women stepped forward in front of the bed, dropped to her knees and kowtowed several times, addressing the prostrate figure on the couch.

Then there was silence in the chamber. The incense was thick in the air and Jack's eyes watered. They waited for a few more minutes but still there was no movement from the figure lying on the bed. When he started snoring, loudly, the young woman moved closer to the bed and cleared her throat. Finally, the man awoke and pulled himself up onto his elbow. His eyes flickered and opened and then, raised from his slumber, the Heavenly King, one of the most powerful men on earth and supposed brother of Jesus Christ – was staring at Jack with big, brown, hypnotic eyes. Jack was mesmerised. He felt as though he was being held in a helpless trance. He remembered the line drawing he had seen in the Edinburgh museum and the portrait on the oil rig of Hong Xiuquan. Jack knew it was the same man. It felt extraordinary to see him in the flesh.

Suddenly, a hand pushed him forward, and Jack realised he should be touching his nose to the ground. He looked around. Backhouse was already kowtowing and Angus began copying him. Jack joined them both on the floor.

"These are the westerners from Shanghai?" the Heavenly King asked. The voice seemed disinterested – as if he couldn't be bothered with earthly matters. He gave a giant yawn.

Backhouse did not raise his head, but spoke into the floor, "Yes, Heavenly Father… they bring the Babbage 'Seeing Engine' and with it great knowledge which we will use in our sacred struggle…"

The Heavenly Father yawned again… and said nothing. Backhouse pressed on, "The First Lord Rengan, General Xiucheng and myself have discussed the matter. We shall take the westerners and the Babbage 'Seeing Engine' to the south… where our great factories are. We shall use their secrets to make new war machines to help in our sacred struggle against the Imperialists."

There was no response from the Heavenly King and then they heard a third giant yawn. Jack looked up. The Heavenly King waved his hand and a bowing girl held out a pipe.

He took a giant suck on the end of the pipe and exhaled black smoke which swirled up to the ceiling. For a moment, his eyes glazed over… then he became cross-eyed and his head fell back onto the bed and he started snoring again.

Backhouse turned to Jack and Angus, clearly embarrassed and said, "I think our audience is over." He kowtowed a final time, and they exited from the fog-filled chamber leaving the Heavenly King, brother of Christ and leader of the Taiping Rebellion, to his own heavenly world.

CHAPTER 14
- THE YANGTZE PRINCESS

The *Yangtze Princess* belched black smoke from a huge chimney sprouting from the middle of its deck as it puffed its way up the great brown Yangtze – the largest river that Jack had ever seen. The boat's steam engine powered two vast paddle wheels – one on either side of the boat – and the relentless pumping of the great iron contraption beneath the deck was starting to inhabit Jack's very soul.

They were up on the deck for fresh air – a privilege allowed them only once since leaving Nanjing. It was a blessed relief from the hot, cramped cabin in the aft of the steamer, where Jack and Angus had been held. Backhouse had taken charge of the precious cargo – the Babbage 'Seeing Engine'. The ship was crawling with Taiping guards and armed with twelve-pounder guns at the bow and aft. No chances were being taken. There were two escort boats – one armed paddle steamer nosed through the great brown river two hundred metres off their bow, and a second followed them from behind.

After they had boarded, Backhouse had attempted to interrogate Jack about the VIGIL device and how it had come into his possession. Jack had done his best to claim that it belonged to his father. Jack pretended that he knew nothing of the function or origin of the device and had assumed that it was some sort of lucky charm. He told Backhouse that his father had never talked to him of Charles Babbage, the CPS or the British government and claimed to be as mystified as Backhouse. With a stroke of brilliance, he suggested the best solution was for Backhouse to find his father as soon as possible. This had made Backhouse think, but so far caused no change of plan. As every minute passed, they steamed further away from Shanghai and his father, and closer to incarceration in the Taiping rebels' heartland in southern China.

"You did well," Angus told Jack as they stood on the deck. Backhouse had hardly given Angus a second thought, though he'd been in the same cabin throughout the interrogation.

"I was squirming as I spun him the yarn about Dad..."

"It sounded believable... but Backhouse is going to keep on until he gets some answers." Angus kicked out in frustration. "We're kidnapped on board this stinking bath tub in the middle of nowhere... time phone's still dead I suppose?"

"I'm not getting it out here, but yes, last time I checked – dead as a dodo."

They stared out at the muddy waters for a while and a gentle breeze gave some relief from the humidity.

"I just had a horrible thought..." Jack said, suddenly breaking the silence.

"What?" Angus looked at him anxiously.

"Well, you know, what if the Revisionist Taurus doesn't work in the same way as VIGIL's. You know how the VIGIL Taurus powers up and alerts the connected time phones every time there is a time signal, so we can time travel? What if the Revisionist Taurus is different – what if it just sits there and does nothing unless there's someone back at the base giving it instructions?"

"Then we'd be stuck here forever – enslaved by this mad lot. Anyway, your dad wouldn't have come to China unless he knew exactly how he was going to get back."

"True." But the mention of his dad gave Jack another stab of anxiety.

Angus looked over the rail at the massive steam paddles churning the brown water into white froth.

"I suppose we could swim for it..."

"You serious?" Jack said. "That riverbank has got to be at least four hundred metres away. And even if we made it, what then?"

Jack looked around. Their Taiping minders were gossiping to each other, further down the deck, "I guess that's why they don't seem to be taking a lot of interest... they know we can't escape." Jack slumped down on the deck, beaten down by the humidity and the relentless pumping of the engine, and out of ideas. Angus sat next to him and they stared up at the huge iron funnel that belched a continuous plume of smoke which drifted on the breeze. Jack's eye followed the smoke, it was drawn to the stern and then beyond to the escort ship behind. "We're stuffed then."

The words had barely left his mouth when suddenly the funnel of the escort ship rose up about twenty metres into the air like a rocket. It hovered momentarily in the air and fell back onto the deck beneath. It was still upright when it landed.

Then it tottered, tipped sideways and crashed into the port paddle wheel, which disintegrated under the impact. The noise from the explosion hit them seconds later – an echoing boom across the water. Jack watched in horror as, almost simultaneously, the bow of the ship and its stern tipped up, pointing into the sky. Something had exploded amidships with such force that it had detached the entire funnel from its housing and blown a hole so big that the ship was no longer able to support its own weight. With astonishing speed, the entire paddle steamer was gobbled up by the great river.

"What happened? Did the engine explode...?" Jack gasped. But the fate of the escort steamer was no accident, for moments later there was a second huge explosion. Ahead, the leading steamer was ablaze – an orange fireball floating on the water. Suddenly, they saw a flotilla of small boats powering towards them from the shore. Each one was full of heavily armed men, but Jack saw that they weren't Taiping. The steamer came alive and Jack witnessed something that he had never seen before and was most unlikely to see again: a vicar of the Church of England orchestrating a contingent of warriors in an armed defence against a band of bloodthirsty river pirates.

The Taiping took up position all along the deck, mounting their rifles on the rail and aiming at the approaching assault boats, which were closing on them rapidly. Backhouse stood at the bow, brandishing a pistol above his head and screaming orders in Mandarin. His red face had once again turned bright purple. Backhouse barked an order and brought his arm down at the same time. As one, the Taiping loosed their first volley.

Jack looked out across the river. Some of the men in the launches were hit, but the boats powered on, nosing towards them relentlessly. It seemed that the Taiping had the advantage in their raised position high up on the deck of the steamer and Jack was convinced the reckless river raiders could not get on board successfully.

"Who are those guys?" Angus shouted, pointing down in the general direction of the approaching boats.

Suddenly a swarthy Taiping sailor thrust a hefty rifle into Jack's hands. "You fight Imperialist dogs too."

A second rifle was thrust at Angus. "Looks like we've just been enlisted."

All hands on the Yangtze Princess were now focused on repelling the Imperialist raid off the starboard deck – but it proved to be a catastrophic tactical error. A burst of machine-gun fire rattled out from behind them and the Taiping soldiers – rifles still pointing out over the river – didn't stand a chance. The attack came as a complete surprise, and in seconds the full complement of Taiping had been completely overwhelmed. Jack swivelled round. Standing high up on the roof of the main cabin were five men brandishing automatic weapons. Jack couldn't understand how they had got aboard – unless they had infiltrated the crew before the ship had set off.

He looked along the deck at the carnage. Two of the gunmen had clambered down from the cabin roof and were now carefully checking each of the bodies. Any that were still alive were dispatched with a single shot or the swing of a kampilan, which looked like an oversized butcher's cleaver. Miraculously, Jack and Angus had been spared, but the two men would soon reach them. For the second time in three days, Jack contemplated his own death. He peered through the railings and out to the river. The first of the launches had tied up beside the Yangtze Princess and more Imperialist troops were clambering aboard.

Jack nudged Angus, "This looks bad, I say we swim for it..." But Angus suddenly leaped to his feet brandishing his rifle.

"Or we go down fighting!"

Jack looked on in horror as Angus raised his gun at the oncoming soldiers, but before he could pull the trigger, a pistol was pressed into the back of his friend's neck. They did not expect to hear a female voice, speaking excellent English. "Please, put that down or you will hurt someone."

Angus froze and Jack wheeled round. "Please," the female voice reiterated.

There was a moment of doubt in Angus's eyes, but then, defeated, he dropped the weapon, which clattered onto the wooden deck.

"Thank you."

They were now surrounded by the Imperialist river raiders. Jack was astonished to see that a slim Chinese girl of only about eighteen years old and half the size of the Imperialist soldiers held the pistol to Angus's neck. She was dressed very simply, with her straight black hair pulled back into a pony tail, but her stature and the simplicity of her dress were misleading. Jack quickly discovered from her poise and demeanour that she was in charge of the whole operation. And there was something else. As Jack looked into her dark, steely eyes, he realised that he recognised her. She was the serving girl who had smiled at him in General Xiucheng's tent in the encampment outside Shanghai. She had been there during the conversation with General Xiucheng about the VIGIL device.

"You are prisoners of the Emperor of China. You will do what I say. Now... where is it?"

"Where is what?"

The young girl snapped her fingers and one of the Imperial soldiers unsheathed an enormous kampilan. He swung it through the air, bringing its razor edge to a halt one centimetre from Angus's throat.

"We do not play games in the Imperial army. Please tell us where the 'Seeing Engine' is, or your friend will lose his head. Another dead body makes no difference to us."

"I… I don't know. Backhouse, the vicar, er, the leader, he stole it from us. Maybe it is in his cabin… or maybe he has it with him…"

At that moment there was shouting from the bows. An Imperial soldier was thundering down the deck, waving something around his head and yelling in Mandarin. He arrived breathless and deposited something in the hands of the girl and then gave a little bow. The girl cradled the object in her palm. It was the VIGIL device. She looked down at it and her face lit up in wonder.

"We have it." She looked at Jack, "You will help us to reveal its secrets. This is the day the tide turns against the Taiping barbarians."

She held the device above her head and shouted something in Mandarin to the soldiers all around. There was a spontaneous outburst of cheering and shots were fired into the air.

Angus glanced at Jack. "Looks like we've just swapped one bunch of lunatics for another."

CHAPTER 15 - SHU-FEI

The girl was called Shu-fei and, having left the confines of the paddle steamer, the party was now on horseback.

Shu-fei kept up the same punishing pace for nearly a whole day – and Jack was not used to it; his whole body was starting to ache. Occasionally they would stop for a gulp of brackish water or a handful of rice. But then they would be off again. No information had been given to them about where they were going or what would happen when they got there. But Jack thought they were travelling north. At this rate they would be riding all the way to Beijing. That morning they had left the low rice paddies in the broad Yangtze plain. It was a war-torn wasteland. Armies had crossed and re-crossed the land, devouring it like vultures picking clean the corpse of a decaying animal. Now though, Jack sensed that the landscape was changing and, in the dwindling afternoon light, he could make out a low ridge of rocky hills. Shu-fei was driving straight towards them.

An hour later, they joined a narrow woodland path and Shu-fei finally eased the pace. They dismounted but carried on walking, leading their horses. After a while the path passed through a broad, square gateway. It was decorated in Chinese writing and had two roofs one above the other, each with upward-pointing eaves. The path wound on, passing through another gate and then over a beautiful, steeply arched bridge. It crossed over a lively brook that splashed down through the woodlands, splitting apart and then re-joining to form a small island. The bridge led onto the island, and to a small, open pavilion that had a pointed roof with six concave, tiled panels. The eaves curled up so far at the edges, that they pointed directly up into the darkening sky. Shu-fei entered the pavilion and sat down on one of the benches that looked out to the water rushing away down through the woods. At last, there was a sense they might be able to stop for a little longer.

Shu-fei spoke. "We rest here for a minute. Then we climb." She turned to one of the swarthy Imperialist warriors and said something. The remains of their food was quickly distributed amongst the small group.

Jack slumped onto one of the benches.

Shu-fei handed him her bottle. "Drink. "She looked at Angus who sat beside them. "We have covered many miles. You have both done well," she said with a twinkle in her eye, "for two barbarians from England."

Jack didn't have the energy to respond, but he noticed that Shu-fei seemed a little more relaxed now. Maybe it was because of the distance they had put between themselves and the Taiping. Though, given the importance of the VIGIL device, Jack expected that the Taiping must already be on their tail.

"You will help us," Shu-fei said suddenly, looking down at the stream.

"What?" Jack said.

She had fire in her eyes. "You will help us. The Imperialists have their faults, but the Taiping are worse. They kill, they destroy, they are like cancer eating the land. We need your help to defeat them. This device, this Babbage 'Seeing Engine', I have heard rumours before of its existence and its powers. I was in General Xiucheng's tent… I saw their reaction… their excitement. Now we have the Engine and we have you. You will show us how it works and you will help us use its secrets to defeat the Taiping." Shu-fei was breathing heavily – she had worked herself into quite a frenzy. "Enough talk," she said finally, "we must climb."

The path snaked on up through the woodland, getting steeper and steeper. It led through a series of ornate gateways to a clearing with views down to the plain below. The scene had taken on a pink hue in the setting sun, but there was little time to stop and admire the view. The path crested a rise in the woodland and opened up into a glade. Ahead, was another gate, behind which stood a small temple. Cliffs rose up behind the temple and Jack saw that the path did not stop there. Instead, it passed the temple and then rose up the cliff on a series of elevated wooden walkways built on timbers jutting out from the cliff face. In some places the path widened into larger wooden platforms extending from the cliff face, supported by long poles underneath or suspended from above. There was a whole network of walkways, platforms and interlinking stairs covering the rock face and leading up to the summit. Jack could even see windows built into the rock face and accessed from the walkways. It looked like a whole vertical village.

Shu-fei wasted no more time. "The horses will be left here and we will climb."

Moments later, they were clambering up the walkways which at some points were only two planks wide. Jack could see through the gap in the planks all the way down to the valley below. There wasn't much protection on the open side either – just a rotting piece of rope linking the occasional fence post. Up they went, higher and higher, and when they finally reached the top, Jack breathed a huge sigh of relief.

The views of the great plain below were breathtaking from the top. Up ahead, there was a monastery and Jack could see distant figures of the Buddhist monks in their flowing saffron robes. Shu-fei hurried them on until they reached a rocky outcrop at the top of the mountain. It was connected to a second outcrop by a rickety bamboo and rope bridge. They followed Shu-fei onto the bridge. Jack felt it swing under his feet and heard the bamboo and rope creaking under his weight. It was getting dark now and he was thankful he could no longer see to the bottom of the chasm between the rocks. He ignored the rush of the waterfall below and looked straight ahead, quickening his pace.

On the other side there were more dwellings: decorated pavilions and pagodas – a whole village built in and around the rocky outcrop. The buildings looked so fragile and delicate that it seemed one strong blast of wind might pluck the whole lot from the mountain and dash it into the Yangtze far off to the south.

Jack felt his legs were finally about to give way when, suddenly, Shu-fei gave a little yelp and darted forward. He watched her run ahead across some paving stones towards a low building. A man was walking towards her and within a few seconds Shu-fei was in his arms. The man lifted Shu-fei from the ground and spun her round in the air in delight. He put her down and when Shu-fei turned, Jack saw that she had tears in her eyes. The man walked towards Jack and Angus but glanced back at the girl. "I got your message from the scout you sent. And these are the Englishmen?" he said. "You have done well, little one, very well."

Shu-fei blushed.

Jack studied the man carefully. He wore a loose-fitting blue jacket with a red border and white piping and black leather boots over white breeches. He had a long black pigtail and a round hat with an upturned-rim which topped a deeply tanned face with thick features. But the most striking of all was the man's size. He was absolutely enormous. Well over two metres in height, Jack reckoned and he wasn't just tall, but wide as well – his shoulders were more than twice as broad as Angus's. He was a giant.

Shu-fei turned to Jack and Angus and announced, "This is Ts-an-ling Lai. Colonel Lai." For the first time Shu-fei's face opened into a broad grin. "My father."

Colonel Lai's voracious appetite matched his enormous size. He had already consumed several bowls of rice and a whole chicken and more food was on the way. They sat around a low table on cushions on the ground. Members of Colonel's Lai's staff waited on them. He had brought them with him to the rendezvous. As they ate, Shu-fei went through the events of the river ambush for the third time. Lai asked incessant questions and seemed to want to know every detail.

"… And you were not followed, little one?"

"The two escort ships were completely destroyed. We executed all the remaining sailors aboard the Yangtze Princess. No survivors."

Shu-fei said the words matter-of-factly, displaying no emotion.

"Good, little one, that is good…" But Lai still seemed unsure and worry lined his face. "But that has only given us a day at most. They will pursue us…"

"But how, father?"

Lai grunted, "These peasants have no loyalty. They have learned to know better. They are loyal to whichever army is passing through their land and who can blame them? No, the secret device you have taken is so valuable that Xiucheng, Rengan and their Taiping animals will strike northwards after us as soon as they can."

"But here? We are in Imperial territory?"

"Imperial territory today, Taiping territory tomorrow. Our armies are weak, they fall back every day. I do not like to admit it, but the Taiping are better disciplined, stronger and they have better weapons. Thanks to the missionary rat, Backhouse, and the secrets he has brought from England…"

Shu-fei shrugged, "At least he is now at the bottom of the Yangtze."

"Good. And with this 'Seeing Engine' we can build better weapons…"

Lai reached beneath the folds of his tunic and removed the VIGIL device which Shu-fei had passed to him earlier. Tentatively, he placed it at the centre of the table.

Lai looked up at Jack, "You will show us its secrets…" Jack didn't want to disappoint this monster of a man. "Yes, well…" he stuttered.

"They will, father, in time." Shu-fei confirmed. "They were taken prisoner by the Taiping; they have lost their father; they have seen the Taiping's ways…They will help us…" Shu-fei turned to Jack and her eyes flashed. "We are the last chance for the Imperialists and delivering this to the emperor will bring us great reward."

Lai added, "But we must take care because the emperor is weak. Some say that he is dying. There is plotting and treachery at court in Beijing. Powerful people vying for position. That dog, Sushun, is the worst. He will do anything to gain power…" he looked at Shu-fei, "He is jealous of Yi, your half-sister, and her influence with the emperor. We must be very careful."

Shu-fei nodded knowingly. Jack did not really understand what Lai meant, but it sounded as though there were divisions amongst the Imperialists, and that Lai and Shu-fei had powerful enemies. It also sounded like they really were on their way to Beijing, and that the Imperial City would be no safer than Shanghai.

Lai heaved himself up onto his feet, "Now, we must rest. Tomorrow, we travel early to the Imperial fort north of here and then onwards to Beijing." He turned towards Jack and Angus. "I am glad you have agreed to help us. Your reward will be great. I have no quarrel with your people. My only quarrel is with the Taiping…" he thought for a moment and then spat, "and Sushun."

It was dark as Shu-fei led them to the little house across the square where the three of them would sleep. The temperature had dropped and a crescent moon, framed by a thousand bright stars, was rising in the sky. As Jack's eyes adjusted to the darkness, he could just make out the silhouette of the temple below. He was tired, but at least his stomach was full, and there was some comfort in the way Shu-fei seemed to have warmed to them after her father's welcome.

"Your father – he is a Colonel in the Imperial army – but he speaks English very well. And your English is perfect, Shu-fei," Jack said.

"My father was a trader. We lived in Shanghai. I have a half-sister from my father's first marriage – called Yi. Shanghai was very busy – many different people came there from all over the world. It is a treaty port. My father learned English and made sure I learned it too. My parents were living in Nanjing when the Taiping first attacked. My mother was killed. It changed my father. He joined the Imperial army and rose quickly through the ranks. But my father hates the Taiping for what they did. And I do too…"

There was fire in her eyes and Jack didn't quite know what to say. "I'm sorry, Shu-fei."

She shrugged. "It is war, Jack. Both sides have done terrible things. I have seen it. But after a while you stop noticing, stop caring. All I know is that we have to win. And you will help us."

If Shu-fei felt any sadness about the death of her mother, she didn't show it. Anything she now felt had been channelled into defeating the Taiping. The only trouble was, the Imperialists were losing the war and the more he learned, the more Jack realised that that they thought the VIGIL device might be their only hope.

It was a cool night and they slept together on mats on the floor. Jack pulled the blanket up around him and tried to get comfortable on the hard ground. He started to doze off, thinking about Shu-fei and her story. She was as fit as an Olympic athlete and tough as nails, but like Jack, she was searching for answers.

CHAPTER 16
- THE SKY DRAGON

Jack woke up with yelling in his ears. He sat bolt upright. People were rushing around everywhere. Angus was already on his feet.

"Get up!" He sounded agitated. "What is it?" Jack stood up slowly.

"The Taiping – they're here. There's a big raiding party out in the valley. They've got motorised transport, big guns, there's a whole bunch of them…"

A huge figure loomed in the doorway. Colonel Lai. He barked orders in Mandarin and then in English.

"We will leave a detachment here to delay them. The rest come now. Hurry!"

They raced to the bamboo and rope bridge – but it was already too late. The monastery complex was swarming with Taiping and the vanguard were making their way up the rocks opposite and over the bridge like a line of army ants.

"No good. This way!" Lai shouted, looking across at the fast-advancing rebels. "We will use the ladders on the other side of the rock to escape…"

Jack looked on as more and more Taiping charged onto the precipitous rope bridge. The first of them were now two-thirds of the way across the bridge and starting to shoot. Their fire was instantly returned by Lai's men, stationed at the end of the bridge, but they were massively outnumbered.

Lai seemed to be weighing up something in his head. Suddenly he withdrew a huge kampilan from his belt. He swung it high up into the air and rushed forward pushing past his soldiers. The blade glistened momentarily in the early dawn light and then he brought it crashing down on one of the rope suspension lines that held up the bridge. It snapped instantly and the whole bridge slewed to one side. He slashed down again on the opposite rope and it gave way. With the two main suspension ropes gone, all that was left was the bamboo walkway and it could not hold the weight of all the men. The bridge collapsed into the gorge taking a contingent of the Taiping rebels with it.

"That gives us some time. Now we go to the ladders. Come." Lai announced, turning away.

If Jack had thought the walkway up to the monastery was scary, the rope ladders which hung off the opposite side of the rocky outcrop were much worse. They looked as if they had not been used for years. Some rungs were rotten, and others were missing altogether. Jack tried to keep in mind one thing... if they held Lai's weight, they would probably hold his. He took a deep breath and plunged over the lip of the rock working his way down the ladder as quickly as he could. Twenty minutes later they were all at the bottom. Jack looked up, but he could not see the top of the outcrop through the tree canopy above them. A further contingent of Lai's men met them at the bottom, with horses, saddled and ready to go.

After two hours' hard riding they arrived at an Imperial guard post. A gate in the wire fence was opened and they passed through it. A rough track wound up a small hill, and as they crested the rise, Jack looked down on a low, wide valley. Below, he saw an Imperialist encampment fortified with a wooden stockade. At the centre of the stockade was a completely flat, bare patch of land, on top of which sat something quite extraordinary. Jack and Angus had seen an array of strange man-made technology on their journey so far, but out of all those strange sights, there was one sort of technology that had been missing. Aircraft. Jack suddenly realised that this was how they were to make the final leg of their journey to the Imperialist heartland, in the far to the north of China.

Looking down from their elevated position, Jack estimated that the structure must have measured two hundred metres from end to end. It was over thirty metres high. It looked like a huge cigar – with a stubby nose at the front and huge, elongated fins at the rear that tapered out from the main body. It was a massive airship – a Zeppelin – and it hovered just above the ground, tethered by cables that were secured to gantries on the landing area. Unlike the Zeppelins that Jack had seen in books and films, this one was highly decorated. It had a vast, scaly, golden dragon painted all along the side, with huge claws extending from its feet and fire bursting from its mouth. Jack counted five gondolas suspended beneath the airship. There was one quite near the front, two smaller ones mounted in parallel about halfway along and another two towards the rear. The first gondola was the largest, but they all had windows at the front of the cabins and propellers at the back. They looked tiny in comparison to the giant airship and Jack realised that, despite its gargantuan size, the whole massive structure might carry only a handful of passengers. On the roof of the airship, quite near the front, Jack saw two figures standing next to two mounted guns. You'd need an incredible head for heights up there.

They pressed on across the valley floor towards the Zeppelin. One of the soldiers prodded Jack in the ribs and they pushed on towards the landing area.

Shu-fei turned to Jack and a smile crossed her lips as she saw Jack and Angus's awe-struck expression.

"You like it, Jack? You like our 'Sky Dragon'?"

Jack wondered if he was the only one who knew that although the mighty structure before them appeared to be an invincible behemoth – in reality it was fragile and vulnerable.

The guards around the encampment were nervous, judging by the speed with which final preparations were being made. They knew that the Taiping would not be far behind.

In a moment, Jack was being hurried up a small stepladder into the front gondola. His breathing quickened. The command gondola was split into two sections. There was a command bridge at the front with windows, and a cabin behind it which was accessed by an open metal walkway, with guns fitted at each side. They were led to the rear cabin and told to sit on the ground at the very back amongst some boxes of supplies. Behind his head Jack heard a loud mechanical thumping as one of the engines shuddered into life. There was shouting from the bridge and then he felt a lurch in his stomach.

They were going up.

CHAPTER 17
- HOT PURSUIT

They had been travelling for over two hours and Angus wasn't feeling too great. Jack was giving him a potted history of airships.

"I think Zeppelins like this were used in the First World War by the Germans to drop bombs on London... and there's something else."

"I can tell this isn't going to make me feel any better..."

"Probably not," Jack continued undaunted. "They get their buoyancy through using gas inside the huge balloon bit up there." Jack jerked his thumb at the ceiling. "Helium was the ideal gas, I don't know what this one uses, but the German Zeppelins used hydrogen. Trouble was, hydrogen is flammable... it explodes..."

"Great..."

"I saw a film on YouTube of the Hindenburg – the biggest Zeppelin ever built – when it came in to land in New Jersey, just before the Second World War. It caught fire... you should have seen it." Jack made a gesture with his hands. "Boom! In less than a minute the whole thing was completely burned to bits. This one looks identical."

"So basically we're trapped inside a gigantic bomb. Any useful suggestions as to how we get off?"

"Only the obvious one, but I checked it an hour ago."

Nevertheless, Jack reached into his undervest and pulled out the time phone. He was so used to it being dormant that it took him by complete surprise when he saw the tell-tale yellow light burning brightly.

"The time signal!"

"At last. Let's do it."

But they were not quick enough. Bullets suddenly ripped into the thin metal skin of the gondola and whipped past their noses, creating a matching pattern of holes on the opposite side as they exited. It was a miracle that neither Jack nor Angus was hit. Jack dropped the time phone in surprise and it spun into corner of the cabin.

Angus leaped forward to try and retrieve it.

They heard screaming orders and clattering feet. Suddenly, there was a staccato ripping sound – like tearing Velcro – as one of the onboard machine guns opened up. From the forward area, they heard the sound of shattering glass and before Angus could recover the time phone, Colonel Lai crashed through the door. His face was badly cut.

"Taiping air attack! We need your help. Follow me."

Lai led them onto the open metal gantry between the front and rear cabins of the forward gondola. The cold air stopped Jack in his tracks. It was like stepping into a freezer. Directly ahead, an airman was swinging the mounted machine gun in an arc from bow to aft along the starboard axis, straining to spot the next incoming Taiping aircraft. Behind him, a second airman lay slumped over the railing of the gantry next to his gun which was at a useless angle.

Jack looked down over the metal gantry. The last time they had crossed between the two gondolas, the Zeppelin had been hovering only a metre from the ground. Now they were a thousand metres up in the sky and there was nothing between Jack's feet and the abyss except a centimetre of latticed metal. Jack froze. Lai pushed him forward.

"Go!" he commanded.

Jack closed his eyes and stepped forward, with Angus following quickly behind him. They approached the body of the airman who had been hit in the first attack and was now slumped over the railing. Lai conducted a cursory inspection of the unfortunate man. He was still breathing – but only just. A pool of blood was spreading across his back – caused by the exit wound from a bullet. Lai grunted, then grabbed the man by his legs and bundled him up and over the gantry railing, tossing him over the side as if he was a sack of potatoes.

"Too much weight," Lai said and ushered Jack forward into the front cabin of the command gondola. The place was a mess. The front windows had been shattered and shards of glass lay everywhere. There were three bodies on the floor.

Lai pointed at Angus. "You help here… Shu-fei will show you what to do," he said, then pointed at Jack. "You come with me – we go up."

Lai pointed to a ladder inside the command gondola and began to climb. For a big man, he was surprisingly nimble. At the top of the ladder he flipped open a hatch in the gondola's roof. Jack followed nervously.

"We're going up into the hull."

Lai nodded his head upwards and Jack's heart sank as he realised what the big man wanted him to do. Above the gondola, the ladder continued up into a second open hatch built directly into the bottom of the vast hull of the airship. Jack counted only six rungs between the hatch in the roof of the gondola and the hatch in the bottom of the hull. The only trouble was, these rungs were completely exposed. Despite the attack, the airship was continuing to move through the air, at maybe fifty miles an hour, Jack guessed. It was one thing to hold onto a ladder that was moving at that speed, but quite another to do it a thousand metres up in the sky whilst under attack from enemy aircraft. One slip on a rung and Jack knew he would bounce once on the roof of the hanging gondola and then plummet into the paddy fields of the Yangtze valley, just like the wretched gunner who had been tossed over the side seconds before.

"No wait. Keep climbing. Don't look down," Lai said helpfully.

Jack gritted his teeth and took his first step. His head popped up through the hatch and a stream of icy air hit him in the face. He tried to ignore the intense fear that caused his arms and legs to shake. With a supreme effort he pulled himself onto the next rung, and then the next. He knew he was moving too fast to be safe and he knew that he should place his hands and feet securely before pushing on up to the next rung, but fear drove him faster and faster up through the air until his head and then his body entered the hatch above and he hauled himself onto the metal walkway inside the bottom of the great hull of the airship. He slumped down, panting, adrenaline coursing through his veins. But his journey up through the airship had only just begun.

In a moment, Lai was beside him, dragging him to his feet.

Jack looked around. The metal ladder continued up vertically, about a further twenty metres, through the hull of the massive airship. Jack expected the inside of the airship to be a cavernous empty space – like some vast cigar filled with gas. But of course, that was not the case. The gas was contained in a number of huge cylindrical cells positioned up and down the inside of the airship.

Jack craned his neck. The next stage of their journey would take them up between two of the gas canisters and on through a third hatch that he could now see in the ceiling of the giant hull. He started to climb. In less than a minute he was there and climbing onto the roof of the Zeppelin with open sky all around.

The whole structure was surprisingly broad on top, though it tapered away on either side. It was like standing on the back of an oversized blue whale. Jack turned and immediately understood what Lai wanted him to do. Directly in front of him, was the gun platform he had seen from the ground before they boarded. On either side of the platform were two medium-calibre machine guns resting on tripods. It looked like they could be swivelled around and angled up or down, and there was something else. Lying on their sides under a heap of blankets were the two gunners. One was asleep and the other had his eyes open and was just staring into space –

completely comatose. Black smoke drifted from a long pipe that lay next to him.

Jack could not quite believe what he was seeing. Here he was, a thousand metres up in the sky on the roof of a Chinese Imperial war Zeppelin and in front of him were two elite airmen of the Imperial air force – both intoxicated by opium. At the sight of the two men Lai flew into a fit of rage. He reached down and hauled one of the men to his feet. But the man couldn't stand and it took all Lai's strength to haul him up onto one shoulder in an impressive fireman's lift. Pumped up with anger, Lai staggered from the platform and dropped the gunner down onto the roof under his feet. The man groaned, unaware of what was happening to him. Lai dug the toe of his boot into the man's side and rolled him once and then a second time until the curvature of the airship's roof did the rest. The man slipped from the top of airship and plummeted earthwards. Without delay, Lai stepped back onto the platform and lifted the second gunner. This one didn't even wake up as Lai administered the same punishment. Lai had now thrown three of his own crew off the airship. At this rate, there would be no one left.

Lai grabbed one of the machine guns and started to move it up and around on its fixed tripod.

"You take the other one!" he shouted to Jack and pointed up into the sky.

Following the direction of his finger, Jack looked up and saw in the distance his first sight of the Taiping aircraft. They were biplanes – similar to those used in the First World War – crude contraptions, but deadly all the same. The planes hovered for a moment and then the first one swooped in for the attack. Coming in from the rear, the plane levelled out just above the spine of the airship, its wheels almost touching the skin. Lai wheeled the heavy machine gun around on its tripod.

Jack watched, mesmerised as the plane flew directly towards them along the spine of the airship. He had no idea what to do with his weapon and dropped onto the wooden platform just as the plane flew over their heads. It cleared them by only a few metres. He scrambled to his feet, only to see a second plane swoop in and repeat the manoeuvre. This time Lai was ready and he let rip with a long burst right into the front of the oncoming aircraft. It was point-blank range and Lai could not miss. Jack saw the pilot slump forward onto his controls. The plane dipped and again Jack dropped to the platform – convinced that the plane would crash straight into them. The wheels glanced off the roof of the airship and the plane bounced upwards, catching its undercarriage on the tripods that held the guns and plucking them free from the platform. The aircraft's momentum was just sufficient to carry it clear of the nose of the airship before it spiralled earthwards.

Lai, sprawled on the gun platform, jumped to his feet and looked despairingly at the mangled tripods which had been ripped from their housings.

"No guns," he pointed into the distance, "But the planes are still coming..."

Lai looked on desperately as a third plane swooped in. This time it traced a line starboard of the airship, trying to determine the damage inflicted by the first attacks. Jack watched as Lai opened a wooden case that was attached to the front of the platform. He pulled out a metal toolbox. Lai stepped off the platform and took a few paces forward across the roof of the airship. Then he heaved the toolbox up above his head and turned to where the third biplane buzzed along the side of the airship, just below where he stood. With a blood-curdling scream Lai hurled the toolbox out with both hands at the plane as it zipped past.

Jack was stunned by how far the box travelled, and just for a second he caught a bemused expression on the pilot's upturned face. In mid-flight, the metal box tipped open and its contents – screwdrivers, spanners and spare parts – sprayed out into the sky like a shrapnel burst from an artillery shell. The pilot spotted the oncoming rain of metal and tried to veer away, but he failed. The port wing of the biplane was stripped bare by the bombardment of metal and the immediate loss of purchase in one wing forced the plane to spin violently. A second later both wings snapped like balsa wood under a catastrophic increase in stress and the whole machine fell towards the ground in a mess of wood, wire and flapping canvas.

Lai wasn't finished. He returned to the wooden case and pulled out a very large pistol – a flare gun. Deftly, he popped open the barrel and inserted a sizeable cartridge. Jack looked up as the first plane circled above, seemingly reluctant to re-enter the fray. Lai took aim and squeezed the trigger. There was a loud 'pop' as the flare gun discharged and Lai's arms jerked with the gun's recoil. A parabola of smoke arced across the sky towards the plane, missing it by a good fifty metres, and then continued on until, in the distance, it suddenly flashed into life as the phosphorous mixture lit up the sky. It was a wild and hopeless shot, but Lai was consumed with battle rage and would not stop. "Another!" Lai fumbled in the cartridge belt, popped open the smoking barrel and inserted a second flare cartridge.

This time he steadied the gun for a little longer and mentally calibrated the angle, based on the trajectory of the previous shot. He fired. Jack watched as again the flare laid a smoky trail in a lazy arc towards the climbing plane. The flare climbed and climbed and then seemed to hang in the air, directly above the plane. Then it dropped and made perfect contact with the biplane's fuselage – plopping into the cramped cockpit. There was an immediate commotion as the pilot realised what had happened. The plane veered this way and that as he struggled with the flare fizzing at his feet. Then, suddenly, there was a flash of light as the phosphorous ignited in a blue-white flash. The plane caught fire – and the flames were quickly fanned by the wind. In one minute all Jack could see was an orange fireball utterly consuming the plane. The pilot managed to struggle free of the cockpit but his foot seemed to be caught in some wire and his body flapped about like a rag doll in the slipstream of the falling aircraft. The plane finally collapsed in on itself.

"You can stay here and keep a lookout," Lai commanded, still trying to catch his breath. "Any more planes – you use the speak machine." Lai put a thumb and forefinger to his ear and mouth.

"What? There's a phone…?" Jack said dumbfounded.

Lai gestured to the remains of the gun deck and sure enough there was a metal box with a crude, old-fashioned telephone wired into it.

"Understand? I am going down to check the rest of the ship and help the others. OK?"

"Yes," Jack said, still dazed by the spectacle that he had just witnessed. In seconds, Lai had disappeared back down the hatch, leaving Jack alone high up on the roof of the Zeppelin. Jack looked out into the sky, scanning the horizon in every direction. There were no more planes to be seen. The gun deck was a broken-up mess – but the airship was, incredibly, still intact. Moreover, both he and the raging Colonel Lai were, quite astonishingly, alive.

He sat down on the wrecked gun deck amongst the splintered wood and paused for breath. He could not quite believe what had just happened. He looked around and noticed that the opium pipe was still lying there, smoking gently. He picked it up. It was about the only thing that had not been destroyed or hurled from the top of the Zeppelin.

Jack did not have long to consider his escape, for at precisely that moment there was a bright flash of white light towards the far end of the Zeppelin's roof. For a moment, he thought that a stray bullet from one of the Taiping aircraft must have punctured the skin of the hull, igniting the gas within, and the whole ship was about to blow. But the flash of light was familiar, he realised – he had seen it before. It was the tell-tale energy burst that signified only one thing – a time-travel event. And now, at the far end of the Zeppelin, he could see the figure of a man slowly making his way towards him across the roof. He moved calmly and methodically. In minutes he would be standing right in front of Jack, who was rooted to the spot. His heart was racing. He couldn't tell from a distance, but he prayed that somehow the strange figure approaching might be his father. But as the man got closer, Jack realised, to his horror, that it wasn't his father at all. It was someone else. But what he was seeing was impossible.

Quite impossible. For Jack knew that the man who approached him was supposed to be dead. In fact, Jack had seen him die with his own eyes – murdered by the Nazis in a bunker in France in 1940. And yet it seemed the man walking towards him now was none other than their old enemy, Dr Pendelshape.

CHAPTER 18
- SON OF THE FATHER

Pendelshape grasped a time phone in one hand and an automatic pistol in the other, which he pointed at Jack. He had known Pendelshape as his History teacher first and then, over time, he had seen him become the fanatical leader of the Revisionists. Eventually that fanaticism had descended into madness and Jack had witnessed Pendelshape's rapid decline and, finally, his brutal demise. The man drew closer, and it suddenly dawned on Jack that he was mistaken. The figure before him wasn't Pendelshape at all. The similarity was uncanny. He had the same gait, the same shape of face and the same look in the eye. But it couldn't be Pendelshape. He was too young.

"Jack Christie, I believe," the man said. His eyes were dead and his voice was bitter. Jack took a step backwards.

"Let me introduce myself, my name is Pendelshape."

"But…"

The man sneered. "Yes, I thought you might recognise it. Let me enlighten you. My full name is Fenton Pendelshape. I think you knew my father. In fact, it is because of him that I am here."

Jack was staggered. "You're Pendelshape's son? But…"

"Yes, Jack. You didn't know?" He laughed, but there was no warmth. "I am my father's only son and I am heir to the Revisionist cause. I'm the next generation – the phoenix risen from the ashes."

"But how…?"

"The Revisionist time phones, Jack. All connected. When there is a time signal and the Taurus is energised you can locate all the other active time phones, if you know how. I picked up your signal – seemed strange that there was another time-traveller in 1860s China. But then I thought I saw something when I departed from our base – your images were very distorted from my position up on the platform so I couldn't be sure. But now I know. Seems I hit the jackpot – Tom Christie's only son." Pendelshape looked up at the open sky all around. "I didn't reckon on such an interesting location… it makes what I have to do almost too easy. I won't ask how you got yourself into this mess…"

It seemed there was no way out, but Jack suddenly had another awful thought and he whispered in desperation to himself, "Dad…"

Pendelshape's lip curled. "Your father? There's no easy way of saying it. He's dead, Jack. Your father is dead." He spoke callously. "Revenge for his betrayal of my father and the Revisionist cause. I can't say it didn't give me some pleasure."

Jack felt as if he had been stabbed through the heart.

"I'll spare you the details. Suffice to say, that I tracked him into the future and then back here. It's been an interesting journey. And one that is not yet finished. As you have probably worked out, something very strange has happened. There has been a major change in the historical timeline that has changed the future. I need to find the cause and rectify it. But first I have other priorities."

Jack wasn't listening. His voice cracked, "You've murdered Dad…?"

He felt rage coursing through his veins. Fenton shrugged, as if he had done little more than swat a fly.

"Are you surprised? Your father is, sorry, was a brilliant man. Now he has even discovered how the Taurus can be used to travel to the future. Incredible, really, incredible. But… he caused my father's death. It's an eye for an eye, Jack. So now, he's gone," he paused, "and now it's your turn. I don't need you getting in my way, looking for revenge…"

Pendelshape raised his pistol to Jack's head but Jack's overwhelming rage gave him the burst of speed and strength that he needed. Bizarrely, he still clutched the opium pipe and now he tightened his grip. In a single movement he swung it as hard as he could at Pendelshape's head. It happened so quickly that Pendelshape had no time to react. It was a perfect blow. Blood appeared instantly on Pendelshape's forehead and he staggered across the roof of the Zeppelin. He still held the pistol, but Jack, surprised by the effect of his actions, landed a second blow on Pendelshape's wrist and the gun spun free. Pendelshape lost balance, stepped sideways and then slipped from view. In seconds he was gone, but for him it was not the end. Still just conscious, he managed one final action. It was the one action that could save his life. There was a second flash of white light and Jack knew Pendelshape had activated his time phone just as he'd started to drop to his grave. Jack's exhilaration at victory was quickly overshadowed by the knowledge that his father was dead, and that he would most likely be seeing Fenton Pendelshape again.

CHAPTER 19
- SUB-CLOUD

When Jack finally clambered back through the roof of the command gondola he saw there were shards of glass scattered over the floor and big holes in the skin of the cabin. Incredibly, the airship was still moving, the big engines pumping – propelling them northwards. The only problem was, there didn't seem to be any crew left. It was just Lai, Shu-fei and Angus. Lai and Shu-fei were busy controlling the command gondola and for a moment Jack and Angus were alone.

Angus saw the expression on Jack's face. "You OK? You look like you've seen a ghost…"

"That's not far from the truth."

"What happened up there?"

"I've just had an encounter with a time traveller. Fenton – remember him? Fenton P. – the person on the Taurus activity log? You'll never guess who he is. I thought it was Pendelshape at first. It's not – but it's the next worst thing. It's his son and…" Jack's voice cracked as he spoke, "he got Dad."

"What?" Angus said in astonishment.

"I'll explain in a minute… have you got it, the time phone?"

"Of course." Angus looked around and patted his chest conspiratorially. "It's right here but the signal's gone again… What do you mean – he 'got' your dad?"

But before Jack could answer, Lai had come back over to them and was barking orders.

"There is much damage, but we are lucky, three engines are still working and we can make repairs." He then turned to Shu-fei and said something in Mandarin. He moved over to the smashed front window and peered out from the cabin. Jack looked too and he could see that the weather was getting worse. In the distance there was a broad bank of grey cloud.

"Cloud is good. We can go up and we won't be seen from below. But we need eyes..." Lai looked at Angus. "You will help Shu-fei in front..." He turned to Jack. "You will be our eyes. Come with me."

Lai marched out onto the gantry. He threw open a narrow hatch in the metal grating under their feet. Jack couldn't bear to look down, but when he finally did, he saw something which he had missed the first time he had crossed the gantry. Hanging beneath there was a strange metal capsule. At first, Jack thought it was a bomb. It was about five metres long and cylindrical but had a bulbous nose which tapered to the rear where four raked fins stuck out from the back. The whole thing was attached to the underside of the gantry and tethered by four wires attached to a cable which was spun onto some winding gear. In the front of the capsule there was a hole with a seat in it – a kind of cockpit. Jack's brow furrowed as he tried to work out what on earth the machine was for. Then he noticed something else. On the inside of the cockpit there was an old-fashioned telephone – just like the one on the gun platform on the roof.

Lai straddled the hatch and pointed at the cockpit below.

Then he pointed at Jack.

"You go in the sub-cloud car. If you see anything use the speak machine to tell us. Take a hat and coat. It will be very cold."

With a rising sense of horror, Jack suddenly realised what he was being asked to do.

"No way..." he tried backing away, but there was nowhere to go.

Lai ignored him and handed him an oversized jacket. Then he lifted Jack from his feet and forced him down through the hatch, suddenly letting him go so he landed with a crash in the cockpit of the sub-cloud car. The whole machine and the winding gear shook noisily as he landed. He was facing forward and his head just popped up over the front of the bulbous nose of the car. The whole contraption seemed incredibly crude and Jack was terrified. But things were about to get much worse.

There was a mechanical scraping and the little machine lurched down a couple of metres, swaying dangerously beneath the gantry. As Jack stared upwards, he could see feet through the metal latticework of the grating above and the faces of Angus, Lai and Shu-fei peering down at him. It was like he was being lowered from a huge ship into the depths of the ocean.

"Don't worry, Jack, it is very safe." Lai leered at him through the grate. "Remember, if you see anything... use the speak machine." He gave a toothy grin.

"It'll be fine Jack, and remember, I'll be up front with Shu-fei driving this beast," Angus said.

"Great – that's made me feel better already," Jack replied.

The sub-cloud car lurched down again and in seconds Jack felt his stomach in his chest as the winding gear unleashed the cable and the car dropped like a stone. It was like descending in an express elevator inside a giant skyscraper, except he was completely exposed to the elements. In seconds the sub-cloud car had dropped more than a hundred metres beneath the giant airship and it was still going down. A couple of minutes later the car jolted to an abrupt halt and Jack felt he might now be flung upwards through the top of the open cockpit. He looked up. The airship was way, way up above him and looked like a small cigar silhouetted against the greying sky. Now the attachment cable was played out to its full extent, the airship could easily have been half a kilometre above his head. Occasionally, there was an eerie whistling as the cable caught the wind. Jack dared to peer downwards – he could see hills way out off in the distance, endless fields in every direction and the tracery of waterways and tracks and villages.

Slowly, Jack calmed down and his mind wound back to the extraordinary meeting with Fenton Pendelshape. Could his father really be dead? Every time Jack remembered Fenton's words outrage welled up inside him. Pendelshape must have intercepted Jack's father in Shanghai when he time travelled from the future – just as Jack and Angus feared that he would. But as Jack gathered himself and thought about it more, he realised that they were still in possession of the one thing that could bring his father back. A time phone connected to the Taurus – a time machine. He knew that when there was a new time signal, he and Angus could travel back to Shanghai and intercept Pendelshape or his father before Pendelshape killed him. Jack knew there was hope.

The cold was beginning to seep through to his fingers and toes, burrowing into his bones. He wasn't sure how much more he could take. Again, he peered up at the airship and his heart jumped. It had gone. Vanished. The cable extended way up above him into the sky and then… it just disappeared. Jack couldn't understand it at first, but then he realised that the airship had ascended into the thickening cloud layer above. The great airship was safely hidden from view in the clouds. Jack wished he was back up there in the relative safety of the mother ship.

Ten minutes later and the cold was becoming unbearable and the cloud above was even thicker. He craned his neck to make one final observation – and then he spotted something on the distant horizon. At first it was only a tiny dot and it looked like it wasn't even moving. As Jack stared, the dot became gradually bigger. It was directly behind him and it was getting closer – an aeroplane. Jack grabbed the phone, but his hands were so cold that he immediately dropped it. He grabbed it again and held it to his ear. Nothing. Next to the receiver there was a cylinder. He remembered an old movie where the man had turned a dial to generate power for the phone. He gave the dial a few vigorous turns and suddenly he heard a voice on the other end of the phone. It was like talking to someone underwater.

"Lai!"

"Aeroplane coming, er, about a mile away… bring me up!"

"Wait there."

"Where do you think I'm going to go?" Jack said under his breath.

He looked around again at the approaching aircraft. Now it was getting closer, he could see that this plane was much bigger than the Taiping biplanes and unlike them, did not have two but three sets of wings. He could also see that the fuselage was enclosed. It appeared that this plane was designed to cover much greater distances. The Taiping had calculated the trajectory of the Imperial airship and had set off in pursuit. They were not going to give up. As Jack studied the approaching aircraft, he noticed that in the far distance, other, similar-shaped aircraft were starting to appear. He counted five of them. Now he could even hear the sound of their engines.

Jack cranked up the phone again and shouted. "Get me up!"

"Wait. We are pulling you up," came the calm reply.

"There are more of them… they are going to attack!" Jack was almost screaming now.

The front plane was already buzzing straight past him – it was less than a hundred metres away. Jack was terrified and could only stare helplessly at the huge, three-winged aircraft. Ahead of him, the triplane banked in a long, lazy arc and came back around for another look at Jack dangling helplessly below the airship.

"He's coming straight for me!" Jack screamed again.

This time there was no response from the airship – just the crackling of empty static.

But as the triplane approached, it did not open fire on Jack.

It just swooped past him and then banked round again. It was not attacking, it was just circling round and round like an eagle expertly playing the thermals, eyeing its prey and waiting for the right moment to strike.

As the triplane made its third circumnavigation, Jack suddenly understood what the Taiping were doing and why they had not attacked the hull of the airship itself. It was a vast target and a few rounds straight into its vast belly might have ended in catastrophe. They did not want to destroy the airship: they wanted to force it to the ground – ideally as near Taiping territory as possible. Then they could recover the precious 'Seeing Engine'. They had caught up with the airship, and now they were just waiting. Waiting and following.

Jack felt a sudden lurch and he looked up. The cloud above seemed to be moving towards him as the cloud car was slowly pulled up. But the sky was also becoming ominously dark. It was then he saw the first flash of lightning.

CHAPTER 20
– HEAVY WEATHER

There was a second flash of lightning and a crack of thunder. The cloud car stopped moving up and then, slowly at first, it started to go back down. Jack could tell by the lack of vibrations that his downward movement was not being caused by the action of the winding gear letting out the tether cable. This was something else. The downward movement increased, and then he started to gain forward momentum. Jack instinctively gripped the lip of the cockpit. He thrust the phone to his ear.

"What's going on?" he shouted. But again, there was nothing but distant crackle.

He looked up forlornly for something that would give him some clue as to what was happening far up in the airship. There was another flash of lightning and a clap of thunder – so close that the cloud car shook. Jack looked up to the clouds again, and suddenly he saw the nose of the airship breach the underside of the dark cloud like a vast diving whale. It was still flying but it was also dropping at an alarming rate. As the mighty airship emerged from the cloud, Jack saw a massive breach in one side. Towards the aft of the ship, there was a giant hole and the skin was flapping free. He saw the bared tracery of metalwork – the airship's skeleton – and inside the huge cylinders that contained the gas. The aft section was scarcely attached to the front. There had been a structural failure in the airship – perhaps caused by the turbulent winds in the clouds above. The 'Sky Dragon', pride of the Imperial air fleet, was going down fast… and Jack was utterly helpless.

There was a forest below and he was rushing towards it at speed. He saw the vast airship way in front of him belly flop into the trees, breaking into two giant mangled pieces. Seconds later, the cloud car hit the canopy of a large tree and was dragged forward through its branches and into the next tree. Jack dipped his head beneath the lip of the cockpit for protection. He felt like one of those mad daredevils who plunge over Niagara Falls in a barrel. He closed his eyes and was banged around inside the metal car as it lurched forward. Then the scraping and jolting suddenly stopped and he had the strange sensation of becoming airborne once again. He poked his head out of the cockpit just as the cloud car flew from the last tree canopy and onto a wide brick platform. It landed with an almighty crunch and bounced once. Jack was thrown free and landed on some paving stones just before the cloud car slammed into a wall directly in front of him, then dropped to the ground – a mangled, battered mess.

Incredibly, Jack was still conscious. But he could taste blood in his mouth. He was high up on some sort of elevated stone platform. On either side there were walls with crenulations built at regular intervals. The cloud car had taken out a chunk of masonry from a stone tower a few metres ahead. The surrounding woodland had saved him. It had absorbed the worst of the impact, but the momentum had thrown him clear and onto this strange structure. Jack pulled himself to his feet. He was bruised and bashed, but as far as he could tell, nothing was broken. The countryside around was hilly and there were areas of thick forest. The wall he was standing on was built on the ridge of a hill and it followed that ridge all the way into the distance, rising and falling with the highest contours and splitting the empty countryside into two parts. At regular intervals along the wall he could see towers. It all looked strangely familiar and, suddenly, Jack realised where he was. He was standing on the Great Wall of China.

He limped towards the crenelated tower, passed through it and carried on to the next section of the wall. A few hundred metres beyond, the great airship had flopped down – straddling the wall. It was a mangled mess of textile and metal. Jack's heart sank. No one could possibly have survived the impact. He started to run towards the airship, but a sharp pain in his leg held him back and he winced. Suddenly, there was an enormous explosion, and the whole airship went up in a massive orange and black fireball. The shockwave from the explosion hit Jack seconds later and floored him. He twisted round and looked up – already a plume of grey smoke was rising high into the sky.

He pulled himself to his feet, emotion welling up inside him. Angus must be dead. Ignoring the pain in his leg, Jack forced himself along the wall towards where the mangled wreckage of the airship lay. The gas had already burned out, though he could still feel the intense heat even at some distance.

All that remained was the steaming, smoking carcass of the once mighty airship. Its warped skeleton was heaped over the wall like the remains of a giant dinosaur whose flesh and innards had been picked clean by hungry carrion birds.

Jack limped on towards the scene of the wreckage, more tentatively now, wary of the heat and what he might find amongst the wreckage. Suddenly he saw three figures. They were staggering towards him along the wall, their arms wrapped around each other's shoulders. Their clothes were burned and their faces blackened. But they were alive and Jack could have jumped for joy.

CHAPTER 21
- REFUGE

It was evening when they finally staggered into the village. There was great excitement from the half-naked children who trailed them into the centre, chatting and shouting as if it was a royal visit. News of the huge explosion had arrived before them, and they were met by a welcoming party. The local dignitaries were out in force, and they kowtowed to Colonel Lai. His height and bulk alone would be sufficient to command respect, but the village elders knew they were in the presence of a bannerman of the Imperial army and a captain of one of the mighty Imperial airships which held a mythical status in the north.

Lai wasted no time. He issued orders and they were ushered to a stone building in the centre of the village. It was surrounded by a high wall and had an archway which led to a central court. The innkeeper greeted them and they were led upstairs to a room away from the litter-strewn street. It was the finest room in the place – big and airy, with decorative paper screens.

"Sit down," Lai commanded. "We must see to the wounds first." Jack and Angus sat on wooden stools next to a stone bed. Angus had burns on the left side of his face and his clothing was torn down the same side, where he had been thrown from the burning airship. There were cuts and bruises, but no broken bones. Jack was still limping. He was pretty sure he had not broken his ankle, but it was sprained and he had bad cuts across his thigh, which kept oozing blood.

Lai started to strip off his clothes and told Jack and Angus to do the same. Jack was pleased to be rid of his sweaty, grubby and bloodied clothes, which he had not changed since Nanking. Two young women tottered into the room, dressed in traditional Han Chinese robes. One carried a bucket of water and the other a box of bandages. Jack noticed how they walked – with a sort of tottering sway – and he looked down at their feet. They were tiny and wrapped in tight silk slippers.

Jack's leg wound was washed and dressed and his ankle wrapped in a sturdy bandage. Angus's face was washed and treated with an ointment. The girls worked busily, chatting happily and occasionally giggling at the white bodies and strange faces of their two young guests. Angus was given some loose-fitting grey trousers which came down to just below his knees and blue gaiters which at first he did not know what to do with. One of the girls showed him how to wrap the gaiters around his shins all the way to his ankles. He was then given a loose-fitting white shirt that fanned out around the elbows. Over this, he wore a short, round-necked waistcoat. The outfit was completed with a pair of silk slippers.

Angus stood up and twirled. "I look even more gorgeous than usual."

The girls blushed and giggled. "You look ridiculous," Jack said.

"Imperial brave… very good." Lai smiled.

"Right, now we must eat," Lai announced, and he led them back downstairs to the tea room, where food had been prepared. There was chicken and rice and a mixture of roots and vegetables all washed down with jasmine tea. They were joined at dinner by three local dignitaries and Lai spent most of the meal deep in conversation with them. They spoke in Mandarin, and Jack and Angus were frustrated that they could not understand the conversation.

As they returned to the rooms with Lai and Shu-fei, after the meal, Shu-fei explained, "The village will give us transport… all they have. They will be rewarded."

"How far is it to Beijing?" Jack asked.

"Perhaps a day. My father has already sent a messenger to Beijing to ask for help."

"But we must leave at first light," Shu-fei said. "The villagers are very worried."

"Because another Zeppelin might drop on their heads?" asked Angus.

"Worse – the villagers say that the Taiping are building a base west of here. Only a few days away. They say that there is an airfield and fortifications. They say they have a whole garrison there – and that more come every day."

"The big Taiping tri-planes we saw – that must be where they are heading," said Jack.

"Yes. They will use the base to help make a final attack into Beijing," said Shu-fei.

"And they will now increase their efforts. They will be desperate to capture the 'Seeing Engine'," she added. "They will find out exactly where the airship crashed and send out scouts and war parties to all the nearby villages. We can only afford a few hours' rest and then we must go."

Jack and Angus finally settled down to sleep in a room at the top of the house. It had a huge brick platform bed with a hearth underneath, stuffed with grass and dung fuel. The fire had been lit and smouldered away. There was a chimney in the wall next to it.

"Someone's set the bed on fire," Angus said, half joking.

"Yeah – that doesn't look safe. Guess the fire underneath is supposed to keep the stone bed warm when you're on it. Let's hope we don't end up being cooked."

With Lai and Shu-fei out of the way, Angus took out the time phone. Jack kept a lookout.

"I can't believe it's still in one piece." Angus said.

"But it's still dead," Jack observed.

"A signal has got to come eventually. We just have to wait – and to be ready," Angus replied. "You still haven't told me what happened up there – on top of the Zeppelin. You know, with Pendelshape's son..."

Jack sighed. "It all happened very quickly. There was no discussion really. He had just come to find me... and – "

"Kill you?" Angus said, alarmed.

Jack remembered how Fenton had coolly announced that he had murdered his father.

"Dad," he swallowed hard. "He said he killed Dad, Angus, there was something in the way he said it. He seemed smug, even happy..."

"He really killed Tom?" Angus said.

"Yes. He was out for revenge – and now he wants to kill me."

"Just what we need," said Angus.

" I know, it was incredible. I was sure that the guy we saw in the Taurus looked like Pendelshape. Now we know the truth. He's the spitting image of his father, but younger, it was like seeing a ghost..."

Angus shook his head, "So old Pendelino had a son..."

"But it's not just that. I mean, I don't know about you, but I never really thought Pendelshape was bad – you know, evil or anything. I always thought he was at least trying to be good – or doing what he thought was the right thing. True, he did go a bit fanatical. But seeing him in that bunker back in France, dying in that horrible way, well you wouldn't wish that on anyone..."

"I don't know, Jack, I mean Pendelshape took terrible, stupid risks, he nearly got us killed, more than once and in the end he was out to get us..."

"Maybe... but this one, this Fenton, his son. Well, he's different. You look into his eyes and they're just dark, dead pits. He's twisted. We're dealing with something – I don't know – something evil." Jack paused for a moment. "But there's hope, Angus." Jack reached out and tapped the time phone. "While we've got this, we can bring Dad back."

"Hold on Jack, you're not saying..."

"It's exactly what I'm saying. As soon as we get another time signal, we must go back to Shanghai and stop Fenton before he murders Dad."

Angus could feel Jack's pain. "It will be very risky…"

"So let's risk it then," Jack replied.

CHAPTER 22
- THE WALL

L ai shook them awake, urgently. "The Taiping are coming. They are already near the village, lots of them. We must go now." In minutes they were downstairs in the courtyard of the inn. The innkeeper was already there, together with a couple of servants and the three elders from the village.

Shu-fei ran into the courtyard, out of breath. "They have big motors. We have only a few minutes' head start." She pointed to the far corner of the courtyard and Jack saw something glistening in the lamplight.

"Transport to Beijing."

Angus stood back in admiration. "Nice..."

The machines in the courtyard looked like motorcycles but were quite unlike any kind of bike Angus had ever seen. They were large and heavy with big knobbly tyres and the engine blocks stuck out a good half metre on either side of the central frames. There were baskets hanging off the front of the bikes and on each side at the back, and they had Imperial dragon flags draped from little masts.

"You can ride a bike?" Lai asked Angus dubiously.

Angus looked at the strange-looking machine. "Not exactly a KTM," he said, giving Jack a sidelong smile, "but yeah, I can ride it."

"Good – let's go then."

Angus fired the engine. It sounded like a mallet hammering at a piece of metal – he felt the whole machine vibrating beneath them.

"Got to be a twelve hundred in there… but most of the engine parts sound like they're trying to escape…" Angus said.

"Just ride it…" Jack said.

The bikes burst through the archway and into the main village square, great gouts of black smoke belching from the triple exhausts. They lurched forward along the rutted street. It was cold and dark, but becoming lighter by the minute, and Jack saw the pale crack across the horizon signalling dawn. Shu-fei was ahead, with Lai riding pillion, wielding a great shotgun. Angus had started to get more comfortable with the controls and there was a great roar as they increased speed. Much to Jack's surprise, the heavy vibration in the frame of the bike, which was travelling up through his spine and into his head, seemed to ease as their speed increased. He snatched a look behind. They were well clear of the village and behind them Jack saw the cluster of roof tops catching the morning light. Then he saw lights following them.

Jack thumped Angus on the back. "They're right on our tail!" Angus's response was instant. The engine wailed and the huge bike surged forward. The machine absorbed the ruts and potholes in the track with ease and soon they were racing through a narrow wooded valley with a river to one side. The light was improving all the time and Jack could clearly discern their pursuers. They also had bikes, but Jack counted a couple of crude-looking four-wheeled vehicles too and, some way behind, a detachment of cavalry. Their helmets glinted and pennants fluttered from the tops of their lances.

Ahead, Jack spotted a steeply raked humpback bridge built over the river. The centre of the bridge had a roof held up by elegant supporting posts. Ahead, Shu-fei did not reduce speed and he watched in amazement as she powered the bike up and over the bridge despite the weight of her father on the back. Angus followed and Jack braced himself. The bike hit the slope and they lurched forward. They shot up and crested the bridge, flew into the air and then landed on the track beyond. On impact, the giant front forks compressed fully and then recoiled violently as the bike bounced. Incredibly, they remained upright.

Angus turned round to Jack, a big grin on his face. "He's got it... the boy's still got it..."

"Just keep your eyes on the stupid road."

Their daring had gained them a few minutes, but already the first contingent of the pursuing Taiping were also over the bridge.

The track now started to zigzag its way up a hill. The big bike pounded upwards eating up each hairpin in turn. In minutes, they were at the top. The sun was well up now – a bright yellow ball hanging on the eastern horizon in a cloudless sky. Ahead, Shu-fei slowed and then stopped her bike and switched off the engine.

"What are you waiting for?" Jack shouted.

Shu-fei and her father peered into the middle distance. Across a range of rolling hills, Jack followed their gaze. It was the wall again, the Great Wall of China – snaking endlessly across the hills. Sometimes it was lost behind a ridge or peak but it would then reappear in the distance.

"There!" Lai pointed and Shu-fei nodded.

Jack couldn't see what he was pointing at but suddenly Shu-fei gunned the engine and the bike roared off again. They dropped from the hill into a dip before rising again on another escarpment. The wall loomed up directly in front of them and the track disappeared through an arched gateway below a signal tower. Next to this, a section of the wall had collapsed... or perhaps locals had helped themselves to its precious cladding of bricks and stone. The rubble and mud, which extended all the way from the ground up onto the crenelated walkway four or five metres above, formed a natural ramp. Soon both bikes were powering up through the rubble and bricks until they arrived high on top of the wall and a ready-built road appeared in front of them, stretching into the distance. Jack turned back to look at the neighbouring ridge down which they had just come. A plume of dust wafted over the crest of the ridge signalling the arrival of the pursuing Taiping. They were only minutes behind. "They're still coming..." Jack shouted to Angus. "But I don't think the four wheelers and horses will be able to get up here."

But Angus seemed to be more interested in watching Shu-fei on the bike ahead. "She's good... very good," he was shouting.

"Stop gawping and concentrate!"

Soon they were powering their way along the top of the Great Wall. The crenulations flashed past on either side as they topped sixty miles an hour. The walkway was bumpy and in places overgrown, and there were great cracks and holes, but Shu-fei and Angus, safely navigated them all.

They approached the first signal tower. From a distance it seemed there was no way the bikes would fit through its arched entrance doorway. It was a tight squeeze, but both machines slipped through the gateway, into the signal tower and out the other side. Up ahead, Jack could see that another section of the wall had partially collapsed, blocking the way completely. They would have to drop back onto the ridge, down the hillside through the woodland, and hope to pick up a track at the bottom of the valley. Angus followed Shu-fei, who manoeuvred her bike deftly down the incline, picking her way through the bricks, rubble and mud that had fallen from the wall.

With a bump, they reached the bottom of the ramp and headed down into the forest. Behind them, Jack saw the heads of their Taiping pursuers as they zipped along the top of the wall. They were not going to give up easily. Angus threw the bike down through the woodland like a skier slaloming through the trees. Sometimes the woodland cleared for a moment and they would speed up and then it would thicken again and they had to weave through the trees – both rider and passenger had to bob down, to miss the worst of the branches clawing out at them. Finally, they burst free from the woodland and clattered onto a wide track at the fringe of the forest, with open fields beyond. Shu-fei pulled up in front of them – her face was pink and she was breathing hard from the exertion of the chase.

"Which way?" she gasped.

Lai pointed. "That way. This is the Beijing road. The Taiping will not dare to come further. This is Imperial country."

But Lai was wrong. As Shu-fei revved the engine, a number of the Taiping bikes dropped down onto the track a hundred metres in front of them. There were more than Jack had first thought and he had been wrong about the horses, too. Suddenly the cavalry were breaking from the woodland and forming up on the road ahead.

"Not good…" Lai muttered under his breath.

Shu-fei turned her bike round to face the opposite direction. But there was no escape. Taiping bikers and cavalry were also arriving on the road behind them. They were surrounded.

Lai gave a great roar of frustration. "Let's fight!" he shouted.

Shu-fei put a hand on his shoulder. "No Father – we are completely outnumbered. They will kill us all…"

"At least many will die with us…"

"But Shu-fei will die also," Jack said. "Are you sure you want that?"

Lai grunted, "What then?"

"As long as we are alive, we have a chance."

From either side, the Taiping started edging towards them. With engines still running, Lai looked around, searching desperately for a way out. But there was none.

Suddenly, there was a blood-curdling scream from the woods. In seconds the entire road was flooded with mounted lancers. Hundreds of them. But they were not the Taiping. They had different uniforms – yellow, iron-studded coats which reached down to their knees and conical leather helmets with tall plumes of red horsehair sprouting from the top. It was the Imperial guard – and they had taken the Taiping completely by surprise. Lai whooped with joy. For a moment, Jack couldn't work out what was going on, but one thing was for sure – the new arrivals seemed to be on their side. Some used long, double-pointed lances; others hacked at their Taiping enemy with swords. A few had guns strapped to their backs.

They tore into the unsuspecting Taiping in a yellow blur. Soon, there were Taiping dead lying all around. They hadn't stood a chance; Jack gazed in horror at the primitive brutality of the fighting.

It was over in minutes. The Taiping had taken a grave risk in mounting a raid so far from their forward base into the heart of Imperial territory and they had paid the price. The remaining Taiping were lined up along the side of the road and being forced to kowtow in front of their captors. Jack looked away… he knew there would be no mercy and, sure enough, soon all the Taiping lay dead at the roadside.

After a while, a man rode up to them on horseback. He wore a long black cloak with an elaborate embroidered panel on the front. On his head, was a red, plumed conical hat. and a thin moustache dropped either side of his mouth. He surveyed the aftermath of the battle with apparent satisfaction.

Shu-fei turned to Jack and whispered, "He is the mandarin. He is in charge. The fact that he is here means that we are very important. We will be escorted to Beijing. We are safe now."

CHAPTER 23
- THE DRAGON'S LAIR

Beijing was a city on the move. As they approached on their motorbikes, they passed lines of refugees streaming away from the centre. Men, women and children flooded past with their goods and chattels piled high on carts.

"What's happening?" Jack called over to Shu-fei riding beside him.

"Your British friends, Jack, they must be close to the city by now," she said, turning back to her father for confirmation.

Lai looked down. "Yes. Eleven thousand British and Sikhs under General Grant and seven thousand French under General Cousin-Montauban. They have sailed in a great fleet in their iron ships from Hong Kong. They have taken the Taku forts and Tienstin and now they approach Beijing."

Jack's heart gave a little jump. He felt suddenly uplifted that his countrymen were so close. "But why are they here?"

"To force the terms of the trade treaty. They say that the Imperial government has not kept its promises to open up more Chinese ports to western countries for trade..." Lai said sadly. "We try to resist. But your western friends are too strong – they have better guns, better weapons. We think we are a great Empire, the centre of the world, but in fact we are not. We fight Britain and France from outside. We fight the Taiping on the inside." They wound their way on through the dusty Beijing suburbs.

There were people everywhere. Lai looked across at Jack as he continued, "That is why we need you, my friend. Your 'Seeing

Engine' will make us strong again. I sent word ahead and our friends here at court in Beijing know we have it safely with us and there is great excitement. They are waiting for us." Lai smiled. "You will have an audience with the Emperor of China himself, Jack. It is an honour unheard of for any other westerner."

At last they turned into a vast square. Ahead was an enormous gate built into a towering wall.

"The Imperial palace…" Shu-fei told them, proudly.

They were outside the Gate of Heavenly Peace, which led to the Forbidden City, the centre of the Chinese Empire. Inside, the emperor lived and ruled, served by thousands of officials, eunuchs and concubines. Lai waved them to stop, and they waited. An entourage of cavalry guards were approaching from the gate and in seconds they were surrounded. Lai had told them that the senior court officials were excitedly awaiting their arrival. The mystical Babbage 'Seeing Engine' was to be delivered right into their hands here in the heart of the Chinese empire. But the mob of guards surrounding them seemed like a very unusual welcoming party. Jack caught a flash of concern on Lai's face – this was not what he was expecting. Something was wrong.

"Sushun," Lai muttered in disgust.

"Who's Sushun?" Jack said.

Shu-fei nodded as a man was escorted through the guards.

He wore heavily-embroidered robes. He had a slim, angular face and a thin wispy, moustache. Jack thought he looked a bit like a rodent.

"That's Sushun. He is very close to the emperor – and leads one of the court factions. But he and my father hate each other." Jack couldn't understand the exchange which now followed between Sushun and Lai, but it became increasingly heated and Lai's big face coloured with anger. Shu-fei looked on with agitation. Suddenly, one of the guards took a swipe at Lai with the flat of his sword. The blow caught Lai unawares and he was thrown from the back of his bike, and landed sprawling, across the dusty square. Shu-fei gasped, but Jack and Angus had no time to act. Jack was pulled from the bike and he kicked out desperately. But the guards were too strong for him; a heavy blow hit the back of his head and everything went dark.

When Jack woke up he had a dull ache in the back of his head. He was lying down and as he tried to pull himself up the stabbing pain in his head increased. He tried touching the back of his head to identify the extent of his injury, but he couldn't – he was manacled to some sort of bench, but at least the hood had been removed.

"Easy my lad..." an English voice spoke up from nearby.

"Are you OK, Jack?" Angus was also close.

Jack tried to focus. They were in a small, gloomy room. There was a little light, but Jack was not sure where it was coming from because he could see no windows. Angus was next to him and he counted three men all chained up beside them. There was no sign of Lai or Shu-fei. As Jack tried to make out his surroundings and remember what had happened in the square, his eye was drawn to a strange figure hanging by a chain from the ceiling in the centre of the room. Initially, it looked like he had no hands or legs, but then Jack realised that his feet and hands were bound tightly into the small of his back. His head lolled and occasionally he gave a low groan.

"Don't look, son, it will just make you feel worse," said the Englishman next to him. Jack could focus now and he saw that the man was balding and had enormous bushy sideburns.

"How's the head? I think you took a bit of a blow, but they seemed to have done you the service of fixing you up. These Imps are a strange lot."

"What is this place? A dungeon?" Jack croaked.

"It's called the Board of Punishments," the Englishman answered.

"Are they going to kill us?" asked Angus.

"Not if Elgin and Grant have their way, son," a second man, sitting beside the first, muttered in a gruff Scottish accent. "They'll be positioning the British guns right at the gates of Beijing as we speak. Touch a hair on our heads and our boys will massacre every living thing in the city."

The two men spoke confidently, but judging by the state of the prisoner hanging from the rafters, their confidence was badly misplaced.

"Who are you?" Jack asked.

"Could ask you two gentlemen the exact same thing... not army, for sure, judging by those clothes... and you look a trifle young to be behind enemy lines."

"It's a long story..." Jack felt too tired to even begin an explanation.

"Well, we've got plenty of time. I would shake your hand, but as you can see we are all somewhat immobilised. I'm Sir Harry Smith Parkes – British Commissioner of Canton, but here as Lord Elgin's interpreter. Or was – until we were kidnapped."

"And I am Henry Loch – attaché to Elgin. Delighted to make your acquaintance."

"Are you part of the British army?" asked Jack.

"Yes – we are part of the joint British and French force that have marched on Beijing. The army is here to ensure the Chinese to accept their obligations in the treaty. We formed an advanced negotiating party. But we were taken prisoner by the Imperialists. They have made a dreadful error of judgement," Parkes said. "The emperor thinks that he can use us and the other prisoners here as bargaining chips with the British and French – so we don't attack Beijing to punish the Imperialists for breaking the treaty. But what they don't realise is that they have already tried Elgin and Grant's patience too far..."

Parkes looked them up and down, "And what is your story, gentlemen?"

Angus looked to Jack, expectantly, waiting to see what story he would conjure up this time.

Jack took a deep breath, "Our family are traders in Shanghai..."

"Shanghai indeed? That's a long way from here," Loch said. "News is that the Taiping rebels have taken it. The irony is that our lot have been helping the Imperialists defend Shanghai from the Taiping rebels so we can evacuate our people. Meanwhile up here in Beijing we're about to attack their capital city. A real old mess. We'll soon have to decide who is going to win and rule China – the Taiping or the Imperialists. But please, carry on with your story."

"When the Taiping took Shanghai, it all happened very quickly. We were split up from our father... and captured by the Taiping rebels. I think it was a bit like you said... the Taiping thought we could be used to bargain with the British. There was a missionary leading them – Josiah Backhouse."

Parkes gasped, "Backhouse! You have met Backhouse? Extraordinary! He's a wanted man, you know. The Cambridge Philosophical Society would love to hear what you know about him and the Taiping."

"He's wanted for passing military secrets from the British government to the Taiping," Loch continued. "When we get hold of him, he'll be charged with treason. But how on earth did you get from Shanghai to Beijing? That's a mighty long way."

"Well, the Taiping were taking us south, but then there was an Imperialist raid when we were on the river and we got caught up in the middle of it. The Imperialists caught us and brought us all the way here..."

"What do you think will happen to us?" Angus asked, nervously.

"We wait for the political game to play out. The Imps know they are in a weak position," Loch said.

Parkes continued, "And as Henry says, the British are going to have to decide which horse to back in China. The reality is that the Taiping are on the rise. Thanks to Backhouse their military organisation and weapons are superior to the Imperialists'. There are many in the CPS and in the government back home who think the Taiping are a better bet than the Imperialists too. They are Christian, in a manner of speaking, and at least they are willing to talk to us and learn from the west. The Imperialists think that everyone from outside their world is inferior. We are the 'long-nosed barbarians' – so what do we have to offer them?"

"And there's another thing," continued Loch. "The Imperialists are riddled with all sorts of factions. Endless plotting... it makes them weak. The emperor is ill, he might die, so they're all vying for favour, trying to second-guess who will take over. One of the factions is led by Prince Sushun and another by the emperor's favourite concubine – Yi. She is the mother of his only child. I tell you; Beijing is a vipers' nest."

Just then, the door to the dungeon swung open and light flooded in, blinding the inmates for a second. At the door stood two armed bannermen and between them a smaller man in a round hat with a long, embroidered robe. He pointed at Jack and Angus and issued an order in a high, squeaky voice. They were dragged from the dungeon, bundled upstairs and along a series of passageways. They passed through a gallery with a polished marble floor fringed with statues of dragons with enormous eyes and then out into the open into an expansive courtyard. Ahead a huge double-roofed pavilion rested on a multi-layered terrace. They were jostled on past this building, through a side gate and into a series of passageways and courtyards beyond.

Finally, they arrived in a great hall the size of a cathedral, with a gleaming floor, lit by great wax lanterns which gave off a strong flowery perfume. Directly ahead, there was a dais and a throne, upon which was seated a figure in golden robes. Jack knew at once that they were in the presence of the Emperor of China, the Son of Heaven. He was flanked on both sides by about a dozen figures. Jack recognised the man to the immediate right of the emperor: it was Sushun – the man who had argued with Lai outside the palace and had flung them into prison. There was a tremendous crashing of gongs as they reached the steps below the throne. Jack felt someone forcing him to his knees and then knocking his head to the marble floor. It didn't make his head feel any better. Out of the corner of his eye he saw Angus get the same treatment.

There was another great roll of drums and a crashing of gongs, and off to his right, Jack saw someone carry forward a low table and place it near the throne. Jack felt his head dragged up by the hair so that he was now looking directly at the emperor. The great man was quite young and pasty-faced. Jack felt fearful of what might happen next, but the young man enthroned before him seemed rather bored by the proceedings. It was all strangely reminiscent of the brief audience with Backhouse and the Hong Xiuquan, the leader of the Taiping, back in Nanjing.

One of the eunuchs flanking the throne called out in good English, "The prince Sushun has done the empire a great service by bringing us a Babbage 'Seeing Engine'..." Jack saw Sushun smirk, and then the eunuch commanded Jack directly, "The emperor now wishes you to reveal the secrets of this magical engine..."

Out of the corner of his eye Jack noticed a small procession of robed eunuchs. The front one held out a purple velvet cushion upon which the VIGIL device was placed. An assistant, walking next to him, carried a parasol over the cushion, shading the device. It was a bizarre sight. The device must have been taken from Lai in the fracas outside the palace. Now it had been presented to the emperor, who wanted Jack and Angus to reveal its secrets. Jack felt a sharp poke in his back as he was bundled forward towards the table where the device now lay. It looked ridiculous sitting on its velvet cushion, shaded by a little parasol, in the vast cathedral-like hall.

Jack looked around and felt twenty pairs of eyes boring into him. But he wasn't quite sure what he was expected to do. Which of its secrets was he supposed to reveal? Depending on which app you had loaded, the device accessed endless information on history, culture and, most importantly, on technology – military technology, in particular. But even if he was to look up, say, 'aeroplane', there was a vast chasm between showing the emperor images of powered flight and the reality of actually building an aeroplane. You would need the right materials – a whole supply chain – scientists, engineers, factories... Jack knew that science and technology, like art and literature – or history itself – were built on what had gone before.

It was a carefully constructed layering process. Through time, ideas and technology were developed, tried and tested, discarded or modified and refined. You couldn't just show someone a picture of a rocket and expect them to build one the following day. In nineteenth-century Britain, with its head start in the industrial revolution, you might have a better chance... Babbage and the CPS had something to work with. But here in China, even though some of the new science had seeped through, it would be much harder. Jack also knew that if he was unable to give these people what they wanted... well, he had seen the man trussed up in the dungeon. He knew what he could expect.

As Jack picked up the device there was a sharp intake of breath from the assembled grandees. They watched in awe as Jack manipulated the mysterious device. He glanced up – the fat eunuch next to him had piggy eyes and was sweating. Jack realised that if he did not deliver, then the eunuch was probably in trouble too. He felt his pulse quicken. What was he to do? What secret should he show them first? As Jack moved his finger over the touch screen, he noticed something. The tiny power bar in the top right corner had only one blob left. Then, quite suddenly, it had no blobs left at all and a helpful message popped onto the screen:

"Goodbye."

The battery was dead. "Great," Jack muttered.

In the palm of his hand Jack held the secrets of history, technology and civilisation. Revealing those secrets was probably the only way he and Angus could buy a little more time in this alien world. But the device had decided to run out of battery. How could something so powerful be rendered useless so easily?

Instinctively, he looked round for a power socket and charger. But then he realised how stupid that was. Of course there were none. He held the device up to see if it might gain some charge from the light through its solar cells. But it was too dim. Jack could have screamed in fury and frustration. But there was nothing he could do. He turned to Angus with desperation in his eyes and gave a little shrug. He looked up at the emperor and shook his head. What was he supposed to say?

"It's not working. We need to charge it. With electricity. It should be possible – but we need to find a power source, or a bright light for a while. Sorry. Your... er... Majesty."

There was a sudden, furious chattering amongst the emperor's advisors as Jack's words were interpreted and translated. Jack looked on and for a moment he was sure he saw the mighty emperor stifle a yawn. Bizarrely, he, for one, didn't seem to care a jot.

After a while a man in flowing red robes stepped forward and pronounced, "You will make it work now!"

"It's not that simple..." Angus suddenly blurted.

"Enough!" one of the others screamed. "Now you will now learn what happens to those who defy the emperor!"

With no further ceremony, Jack and Angus were dragged to their feet and bundled from the great hall, back out into the courtyard. Jack's heart was racing. He didn't know what was coming next, but the image of the man hanging from the ceiling in the dungeon flashed through his mind. He started to struggle, but his hands were quickly tied and once again the hood was slipped over his head. As they were jostled and pushed along, he could hear Angus beside him complaining bitterly. He soon became disorientated as they made their way this way and that back through the maze of the Forbidden City.

Then, quite suddenly, they came to an abrupt halt. Jack had no idea where they were. There were voices and then a long discussion in Mandarin. They stood for a little while and Jack strained to hear, trying to get some clue as to what was going on. The inside of the hood that Jack wore was clammy and wet from his own breath. After a few minutes, they moved on. But this time, Jack felt an arm around his shoulder, guiding him. The hand felt different, it was firm, and not aggressive. They rounded a corner and stopped for a second time. He felt a change in the surroundings – there was more bustle and noise and his hood was catching a little in the breeze. Suddenly, his hands were lifted up and a sharp blade sliced through the cord that bound them. Next, the hood was eased off his head. It was clear they were no longer inside the Forbidden City. Jack blinked in the daylight and saw Angus blinking too. Directly ahead stood the towering figure of Colonel Lai and next to him was Shu-fei. They were both smiling.

CHAPTER 24
- YI CONCUBINE

Within an hour, they were well beyond the city walls. "We will be safe now," Lai said.

"What happened, Shu-fei? How did you manage to rescue us?" Jack asked.

"Sushun distrusts my father because his first daughter... my half-sister... is Yi Concubine – the mother of the emperor's only child. My sister has the emperor's ear and is very powerful because she is mother to his heir. When Sushun heard we were bringing the 'Seeing Engine' to Beijing he saw an opportunity. He managed to get us arrested and you put in prison. He wanted to gain the credit for himself and take possession of the Engine. But my half-sister Yi found out and got us released. We also got the Engine back."

"Always fighting amongst ourselves... this is why we are weak," Lai said sadly. "But one day I will kill that dog Sushun, I swear."

"So where are we going now?" Angus said.

Shu-fei smiled. "You'll see..."

They rode down to a lake, which was crossed by a raised causeway leading to a gate. Two uniformed guards greeted them at the gate and there was a short discussion with Lai. They were then escorted through the gate and into the gardens beyond. It was as if they had arrived in some mystical fairyland.

"The Summer Palace," Shu-fei announced. "Not a Palace really – it's more of a gigantic garden. It goes on for miles."

Jack was speechless. Stretching before them was an astonishing, breathtaking world of gardens, lakes, fountains, pavilions and temples. Jack had seen the Taiping capital, Nanjing, a Buddhist monastery built into a mountain, and even the Forbidden City itself… but none of it, nothing he had ever seen, compared with this. Man and nature had come together in perfect harmony in a blended palette of colours and shapes.

Lai grinned at the astonishment on Jack and Angus's faces. "It has taken centuries to build."

"There are three gardens: the Garden of Perfect Brightness, the Garden of Eternal Spring and the Elegant Spring Garden," Shu-fei explained. "They are five times as large as the Forbidden City… and it is all for the use of the emperor and his court. We are special guests."

As they walked on, Jack realised that there must have been hundreds of structures – halls, pavilions, galleries… all of them extraordinarily beautiful and ornate.

"Famous landscapes from the south of China are reproduced here… the buildings contain works of art, statues, literature…" Lai pointed to the most astonishing building they had yet seen, "that is the Yuan Ming Yuan Haiyan…"

"Bit of a mouthful," Angus said.

Jack stopped and gaped at the palace before them. In front was a fountain surrounded by sculptures. There were steps leading from both sides up to a front gate adorned with carvings. The whole structure was extraordinarily ornate. You would need to stand in front of it for days to properly take in all its intricate features. And there was something else about the building – Jack had seen it before. He nudged Angus.

"POD – Day of Rebellion."

"What?"

"It's the same palace they use in Day of Rebellion," Jack said. "And here we are… seeing it for real."

"You're right," said Angus. "Better watch out for unpleasant horsemen."

After a while, they entered what was supposed to be one of the more modest pavilions. It wasn't exactly small, however, and the roof was decorated with gold leaf. Inside, there was marble, jade and ivory and each room was stuffed with porcelain, jewellery and paintings. There were clothes too – magnificent furs and embroidered silk dresses.

"Every object has its special place," Shu-fei said. "Everything is labelled with its description, origin and the position it must occupy in the room."

They were welcomed by a servant and led to a room in the heart of the pavilion. A young woman stood in the middle of the room. She wore a long, sweeping robe and her hair was coiled on top of her head. She was very beautiful. As soon as she saw them, she rushed forward to Lai and threw her arms around him. Lai spoke to her in Mandarin. Then as he presented Jack and Angus, he broke into English. "My daughter, Yi. The emperor's favourite and mother to the emperor's only son and heir."

Jack turned to Shu-fei; "Your sister?"

Shu-fei smiled and gave Yi a hug.

They stood back as Lai and his daughters engaged in an intense conversation. After a while they stopped and Shu-fei turned to explain.

"More negotiations are underway with the British and French outside Beijing. They are furious that some of their men have been taken hostage. These are the men you saw imprisoned in the Forbidden City – Parkes, Loch and the others. There will be retribution from the British. The latest news is that the emperor is planning to leave for the north, to escape Beijing before it is attacked. He wants Yi to go with him."

Jack looked at Lai and Shu-fei, "So why have you brought us here...?"

"We are safest here for now; together we are stronger," Shu-fei said.

Lai glanced at Yi. "My daughter is a powerful woman – but she is frightened about what will happen to her and to her little son if the emperor dies and Sushun or one of the others takes over." He smiled, "But she is clever…"

"We are in a strong position." Shu-fei added, "As my sister is the emperor's favourite. And now we have the 'Seeing Engine' and the people who can interpret it."

"Sushun and his dogs won't touch us now. They wouldn't dare." Suddenly, there was a scream from outside the pavilion. Lai flashed a look at his daughters. They heard the sound of heavy boots and turned round. In the doorway stood a man dressed in heavily embroidered robes. He was flanked by two Imperial guards. It was Prince Sushun.

"How delightful to see you again, my prince," Yi said, sarcastically, greeting him in English for the benefit of Jack and Angus.

In perfect English, Sushun replied gruffly, "The emperor is travelling to Jehol. He has instructed you, Yi Concubine, to join him." Then he addressed Lai, "And as for you, pig dirt, orders have been issued for your arrest – for treason – we want the 'Seeing Engine' back." He then pointed at Jack and Angus. "And these two are my prisoners. They will return to the Board of Punishments."

Lai's response was instant. He removed the VIGIL device from his coat, threw it to Shu-fei and spoke to his daughters.

"Run – little ones – take them to safety… I will deal with these dogs once and for all."

He took his sword from his belt and advanced on Sushun and the two guards.

"Father!" Shu-fei cried.

"Go!" he shouted.

Shu-fei, Yi, Jack and Angus fled from the pavilion just as Jack heard the first clash of sword on sword behind them. In a moment they were outside and running through the ornate maze of paths, hedges, bridges and lakes. Shu-fei pushed them on at a heartburning pace. Suddenly, the earth seemed to tremble beneath them. They glanced round – a posse of Imperial cavalry had spotted them and were tearing after them through the gardens. One was galloping through a lake that fringed the lawn leading down from the pavilion, water spraying up from the horse's hooves. Yi took the lead, directing them off the main path and into a narrow, hedged passageway. Beyond there was a wide grass bank, which rose gently to the palace they had seen earlier – the Yuan Ming Yuan Haiyan. They climbed up some marble steps and into the lavish entrance way. But the horsemen were right on their tail. Lining one side of the hall were huge green vases – twice Jack's height and so delicately thin that the light shone straight through them.

Yi paused in the middle of the building, panting. For the first time she did not seem to know what to do or where to go. Suddenly, there was a loud crash. They wheeled round. A huge cavalryman sat astride a muscular black horse at the end of the great hall. He was soon joined by the others. They had ridden straight up and into the pavilion. The lancer's steel helmet glimmered and its long, feathered plume quivered. The horse bucked, and the horseman balanced his lance, a gossamer-thin pole, in his right hand. He dug his heels hard into the flanks of his horse. It reared... and then, it charged. The horseman skilfully manoeuvred the lance so that it pointed at a slight angle down towards Shu-fei, Yi, Jack and Angus. Jack and Angus dived for cover, bundling Yi with them. But Shu-fei was too slow. Jack twisted round and, as Shu-fei fell, he saw the lance pierce her chest. Jack cried out in horror as she slumped to the ground. In one hand she still clutched the VIGIL device, but now her fingers gently unfurled and the precious object slipped from her grasp and slid towards Jack. The horseman withdrew the lance from her body. He steered the horse back and it snorted as the lancer turned round for a second attack. This time he headed straight for Jack, his lance aimed directly at Jack's heart.

Jack was frozen to the spot. The lance was centimetres away when he heard a loud mechanical whirring sound. Bullets from a machine gun ripped into the lancer's chest and he was thrown clear from the horse. As the horseman tumbled backwards onto the marble floor, Jack came to his senses and dived sideways to avoid the horse. The lancer landed awkwardly and didn't move. Jack, Angus and Yi rushed over to Shu-fei. Yi cradled her half-sister's head in her hands. But it lolled back uselessly, her eyes staring up into the gilded rafters of the pavilion.

A second burst of machine-gun fire put paid to the other lancers.

"Stop!"

A British infantry officer advanced from his position at the rear of the pavilion, his gun still smoking. He was flanked by four other men, all with automatic rifles slung to the side of their hips. Sobbing bitterly, Yi was still kneeling next to her half-sister on the floor. A dark pool of blood had formed around Shu-fei's lifeless body. Jack felt a lump in his throat as he pulled himself to his feet.

In seconds, the British officer was at their side and he and his comrades swept their weapons about the pavilion double checking that the lancers had gone.

"My God!" the officer exclaimed.

Jack looked up. The man had a huge handlebar moustache and wore a white pith helmet. It was Captain James Fleming of the Dragoon Guards, the man who had been captured with them outside Shanghai.

"Captain?"

"How on earth…? We thought you were dead," Captain Fleming said.

"Well, luckily, we were rescued… but, what about you? How did you get here?" Jack asked.

"I managed to escape and make my way back to Shanghai. Got out on the last evacuation boat, before the Taiping overran the place. I was immediately sent north to join Grant's forces outside Beijing, and so, here I am. But what happened to you?"

"We were taken north, and, well, we ended up here, prisoners in Beijing," Jack could feel an overwhelming sense of relief welling up inside him. He and Angus had been travelling through China for days now and had barely escaped with their lives. It was reassuring to see the captain again.

"We're glad to see you," his voice cracked. "You saved our lives."

"But what brought you here, to this palace?" Angus said.

Fleming blushed and he looked at his boots. "Advance party – the main British force is a few miles away… we've come here for, er, reconnaissance… "

But as Jack came back to his senses he noticed something strange about the men. Several were carrying extra bags and one had a huge sack thrown over his shoulder. Their pockets were full and, from a side portico, another two troopers who had missed the earlier action entered the main hall. One was wearing two fur coats and the other was pushing a cart – like a giant pram. It was stuffed full of silks, porcelain, jade, gold and silver. "Conqueror's privilege," Fleming shrugged, a little embarrassed. "But no matter – we must return you to our headquarters. It is not safe here."

"No," Jack said, "there are Imperial guards everywhere. In Beijing we saw the British prisoners – Parkes and Loch and there were others…"

This news interested Fleming greatly. "You saw the hostages? This is important. All the top brass are angry about the hostages. It's against all protocol. We must take you to headquarters now to meet Lord Elgin so you can tell him what you have seen."

Fleming barked some orders. There were complaints from the other British troops, who would have to stop looting in order to look after Jack and Angus. As the first into the Summer Palace they had the pick of the place… but from what Jack could see, there was no way they could possibly carry any more. Jack wondered what would happen to the place once the rest of the army discovered the almost limitless extent of its treasures.

"What about Shu-fei?" Jack looked down at her lifeless body.

"A friend?" the officer said. "I am sorry, we have to leave her, it is too dangerous to stay longer."

Jack bent down over Shu-fei. She had rescued them from the Taiping, guided them north and then saved them from the Board of Punishments.

"Yi, I'm sorry…" Jack said, placing his hand on her shoulder. "We must go."

Yi looked up at him. "My place is here… and my father will be here soon. We will survive… we always have. You must go back to your people." She reached out to Jack and opened her hand. In it there was a little black jade dragon, dangling on a gold chain. "Take it Jack. It was Shu-fei's. She would have wanted you to have it. She liked you. I could tell."

Jack took the necklace and looked up into Yi's eyes. "Thank you."

"Come on!" Angus pressed. "We've got to go."

Jack turned away and he and Angus followed Fleming and the other soldiers back down the hallway of the Yuan Ming Yuan Haiyan. Jack was distraught, but as they walked Angus nudged him and opened his jacket. He had recovered the VIGIL device. "And there's something else," Angus whispered. He opened his hand to show Jack the time phone. The yellow light was burning brightly. They had a time signal. At last. "Finally… we have a chance to get out of here…"

Jack's eyes lit up, "First, we need to travel back to Shanghai and get to Dad before Fenton does…"

CHAPTER 25
- THE WILTING POPPY

They stepped out from the shadow of the alleyway into blinding sunshine. The waterfront of Shanghai was a kaleidoscope of humanity: Chinese, European, Indian and African – and they were all on the move. Carriages clattered down from the city into the docks, halting in front of the great warehouses and offloading a steady stream of passengers. A platoon of Indian soldiers in turbans marched up from the harbour, scattering scavenging seagulls before disappearing behind a stack of tea chests stamped 'Liverpool Docks'. Porters scurried to and fro between the carriages and the waiting boats, backs bent double from their loads. Western families, pale-faced and sweltering in their Sunday best, hovered anxiously as their hastily gathered belongings were ferried down to the sea and what they hoped was safety. "Well that's the harbour," Jack said.

"This place is complete mayhem," Angus said, looking at the scene around them. "How are we supposed to find your dad amongst all these people?"

"I don't know. It's weird to think that we were only a mile away on the outskirts of the city just days ago when we got ambushed by Backhouse and the Taiping…"

Out in the harbour, the murky water was hardly visible. Gangplanks ran out from the sea wall and then from boat to boat forming a cobweb that entrapped everything from the lowliest rowing boats and junks up to the fine riverboats with their pagoda cabins. Beyond this, further out to sea, the Union Jack and Red

Ensign fluttered from two sleek gunboats – sentinels at anchor, their decks swarming with sailors and marines, armed to the teeth.

"Everyone's trying to leave the city," Jack said. "Remember what Fleming said – in a few hours' time the place will be completely overrun by the Taiping. The harbour area will be the last place protected by the British." Jack bit his lip in frustration. "We've got to find Dad before it's too late. Let's start working our way down the waterfront hotels and bars."

"What about that big one – the Wilting Poppy...?" Angus pointed across the street.

"OK. Let's try it. But we need to be careful. We know Fenton could be around here too..." Jack added under his breath, "Let's hope we're not too late."

They shoved their way through the crowds and street sellers who hawked everything from soup to flapping paper butterflies on sticks that bobbed and dipped above the crowd. Finally, they arrived outside the double doors of the Wilting Poppy.

"Here goes..."

Inside, the bar was surprisingly large and airy – a neat square room divided into equal thirds by two sets of pillars. The rattan tables and chairs were arranged either side of the room and there was a huge barometer behind the wooden bar. It was busy, and people were taking temporary refuge from the heat and crowds outside – most were waiting for evacuation. There was a lot of noise – women comforted their children and men exchanged rumours of the startling and frightening progress of the Taiping. Many were taking comfort in alcohol at the bar.

Jack scanned the room, desperately looking for his father. Then, in a far corner a man caught his eye. He wore a frockcoat and stiff white collar and pored over a broadsheet, glass in hand, seemingly oblivious to everything going on around him. Jack could hardly contain his excitement.

"Dad!"

He started to push his way forward through the crowd, Angus following close behind. But they had arrived a moment too late. As if out of nowhere, a man suddenly barged past him. Jack tripped and fell to the floor.

"How rude!" Jack heard a cross bystander exclaim. He scrambled up from the ground just as the man marched ominously towards his father. It was then that Jack realised that the man was holding a black pistol. There was a scream and Jack saw his father look up and then jump to his feet in alarm as the man bore down on him. It all seemed to be happening in slow motion but Jack was powerless to do anything. He could not see the man's face, but Jack could tell from his stature and gait that it was Fenton Pendelshape. Jack screamed a warning – but it was too late. Two shots rang out – they sounded strangely muffled in the crowded bar – then there was an incandescent flash of white light. There was a sudden piercing scream, followed by blind panic. Customers and staff hurled themselves through the exits, glasses smashed and chairs and tables went flying. In seconds Jack and Angus were alone in the bar, with a body on the floor: the body of Tom Christie, Jack's father.

Jack looked down, overwhelmed with grief. He reached out, grabbed his father and shook him. But it was no use. Jack felt blood on his hands – warm and sticky – he held his palms to his face and stared at them in disbelief.

"Oh God…"

"Get me out of this damned thing."

It was his father's voice. Jack looked back down. Tom Christie's eyes were wide open. He was very much alive.

"Dad?"

Jack's eyes met his father's and it was difficult to tell which of them looked most surprised.

"Jack? But how?"

"I could ask you the same thing, Dad. How did you survive a bullet in the chest?"

"I've no idea how you got here – but I am glad to see you guys," Christie said. "That was a close shave." Christie tapped his chest, it made a hard, knocking sound. "Thought something like this might happen, I took precautions – Kevlar vest for a start."

"But what if he had gone for your head…"

"He didn't…"

"But there's blood."

"Yes – he got my arm. Need to get that seen to… my pack's over there – there should be a medical kit… see what you can find." He pulled himself up into a sitting position, "I'm going to have some nice bruises, my chest hurts like someone has run over it." He scanned the inside of the bar, "Can't stay here, police will be here in a minute. Ow! That hurts – hurry up – I need a bandage."

Jack and Angus helped Christie to his feet.

"Through there?" Angus suggested, nodding towards the kitchen. "There should be water and stuff – we can try and get you patched up."

The kitchen was deserted. In minutes, Christie's upper arm was strapped up but the bandage was already pink with the oozing blood. It was painful, but thankfully only a flesh wound. He swallowed a couple of painkillers from the medical kit.

"I'll be fine… just need to take a minute here…" he took deep breaths and gradually the colour started to return to his cheeks.

"Drink this," Jack proffered some water.

"Thanks," Christie looked at them both and took another deep breath. "I think we both have some explaining to do … then I think we need to get to work."

Christie spoke quickly as he explained the extraordinary course of events that had brought him to Shanghai. "I'm sorry about the cloak and dagger stuff back at the Bass Rock. I was worried that you might be followed. I'm afraid events then rather overtook us. Fenton infiltrated the base. To be honest, Pendelshape never really talked much about his son, but all along he was preparing for the day that the two of them would take over. Then Pendelshape died in France and Fenton blamed me – and you – he flew into a rage and made his move. He and his two cronies jumped me at the Revisionist base. They wounded me… but I managed to return the favour. In the end it was just me versus Fenton."

"The two men at the base – you killed them?" Jack was horrified.

"Yes." Guilt etched Christie's face. "It all happened in a blur. It was them or me…"

"I'm just glad you're OK, Dad." Jack thought for a moment. "You were injured and Fenton was still after you – so you escaped to the future using the Taurus?"

"Yes. It's something I've been working on. It's why I wanted you to come to the base… the Taurus can take us to the future. It changes everything."

"Certainly gave us a bit of a surprise," Angus said.

"You must have followed me every step of the way. I'm impressed."

"We saw Fenton in the Taurus," Jack explained. "For a moment we thought he was Pendelshape himself – they look so alike. We checked out the Taurus activity logs and decided to follow you both. We got to the base in the future and couldn't work out what had happened. We saw all the ice and the rig and then we found your notes and reran your Timeline Simulation. But it was the activity logs that finally told us you had come back here – and showed that Fenton had followed you. We were worried, Dad, worried about what would happen."

Christie smiled. "Clever… very clever…" He put his good arm around Jack's shoulder. "You guys are good. No wonder VIGIL wants you on their side."

"What I don't get though, Dad, is, what's going on… I mean… what has happened to change the future so much?"

"Yeah – we landed in this weird hardware shop – it had hair-dryers and kettles, and we've seen motor bikes, aeroplanes, lots of weird stuff that isn't supposed to be around in 1860," Angus said.

"We got captured by the Taiping and then the Imperialists." Jack saw the astonished look on his father's face. "I can tell you, we've seen it all – it's a bit of a story how we got back here, but the Taiping have quite modern weapons – and the Imperialist have some modern stuff too… in fact, they've even got a Zeppelin –"

Christie's eyes were on sticks, "A Zeppelin? Incredible…"

"Not so incredible as it happens…" Angus added. "It blew up!" He tapped his face. "See these burns?"

"All this is to do with what we saw in the future – the new ice age we saw – isn't it Dad? That's what you discovered when Fenton was chasing you…"

"You're right, Jack. I got in the Taurus to try and buy some time, to escape. But when I arrived at our base in the future, in 2046, I realised that something terrible had happened. The climate had changed. So I ran some simulations."

"Do you know what happened to change the future?"

"Basically, there has been a massively accelerated industrial revolution. The industrialisation of China and the Far East has happened a century before it happens in our timeline – in 'real' history if you like. That's created more rapid global warming and caused competition for resources – so you get Chinese oil rigs exploiting the Arctic as the climate warms up – but then there is a tipping point, the North Atlantic Drift seizes up and the climate flips the other way. Hence, a new ice age."

"And that ocean pump thingy stops," Angus said. "Just like you said, Jack."

"OK, so what caused China to industrialise early?" Jack asked.

"The simulations I ran suggested something in 1860, right here and now in Shanghai. That's the simulation you saw on my computer and the notes I scribbled down. I thought it was due to the Taiping winning their civil war against the Imperialists, which, for some reason, caused China to industrialise much more quickly. I have only been here in Shanghai for a couple of hours but I already know that can't be right. And you've confirmed it. You say that the technology and the weapons you've seen are all kind of jumbled up. It suggests that something must have happened much earlier than 1860. I'm stuck, Jack, I don't know which event caused the future to change, and unless we can find it, we can't change the future back to how it is supposed to be."

Jack thought for a moment and then smacked his forehead, "I know!"

"What?" exclaimed Christie and Angus in unison.

"I mean I know when it was, the real turning point – the Point of Divergence, when everything changed," he turned to Angus. "Captain Fleming told us…"

"Did he?" Angus replied.

Jack turned to his father, speaking quickly, "Fleming was an army captain we met and he said that it all goes back to a conference. There's something called the Cambridge Philosophical Society – the CPS – a really powerful group of English scientists, led by a guy called Charles Babbage."

Tom Christie nodded. "Yes – I know who Babbage is. He invented the Difference Engine, he's the father of modern computing, he was way ahead of his time."

"Right, anyway," Jack continued. "The CPS ran a conference in 1836 at Cambridge University – Trinity College, I think. This conference was when Babbage and the other leaders of the CPS disclosed a series of new discoveries and inventions. All the top brass in government and the military were invited and apparently it had a massive impact. Fleming knew all about it even though it was twenty-five years ago; he talked about Babbage and the CPS like they were gods. They were called the 'Science Lords'."

"Can you remember when the conference was?" Christie said.

"Yes actually, the date stuck in my head. It was March 31st, 1836."

"You say Babbage and his CPS buddies presented new inventions at this conference... but where did Babbage get the information from?"

Jack grinned, "I think we know that too, Dad."

He brought out the VIGIL device and placed it on the table. "It's the reason we've been chased halfway round China..." Jack said. "But also the reason we've managed to stay alive. None of them really know how to use it... but they think we do and that we can interpret all its information for them. Josiah Backhouse was very excited about how it would give his Taiping friends an even bigger advantage against the Imperialists..."

"Who's Backhouse?"

"Josiah Backhouse. Real weirdo." Angus tapped his temple. "He is with the Taiping rebels, he's English and used to be close to Babbage and in the CPS. He came to China to help the Taiping because they are Christians fighting the corrupt Chinese government. Then he started passing them technology secrets from the CPS... it's one of the reasons he has become so powerful in the Taiping and that the Taiping have had success against the Imperialists. But the thing is, Dad, when Backhouse discovered we had this VIGIL device, he was really excited, he actually recognised it. He knew what it was: he had seen one before."

"We couldn't believe it," Angus added. "He called it the Babbage 'Seeing Engine' – weird name, I know. It's like it's some sort of magic thing. Which I guess it is, in a way."

"But Backhouse definitely had seen something similar," said Jack. "So, somehow, the CPS, and therefore Babbage himself, must have got hold of a VIGIL device, just like mine, in 1836... or maybe even earlier. And that was the source of all their knowledge."

Christie nodded his head slowly, absorbing everything he had just heard. "Babbage was a genius. He also had a skill for taking difficult ideas and translating them into real working machines. There is no doubt that if he had a device like this he could have used the apps in there to design and build some modern technologies. It sounds like that's what he and his CPS mates, including Backhouse, did. Britain already had a solid industrial base and could start to manufacture some of the new inventions... and then they'd have filtered out to the rest of the world." He patted Jack on the back. "You're a chip off the old block." He paused. "But there is still the one fundamental question we haven't answered..."

"Right," said Angus. "How did Babbage and Backhouse get hold of a VIGIL device in the first place...?"

"Well it could only come from VIGIL themselves," Jack said. "Yeah, but why would VIGIL do that – I mean leave something like this in the past?" Angus said. "It's totally against all the rules."

"Yes – and we know why – it's caused a horrendous mess."

"What next then?" asked Angus.

"We keep following the trail back in time until we get to the point where everything changes," Christie said. "Ultimately we're looking for the point where, for whatever reason, Babbage gets his hands on the VIGIL device. From that moment on, everything starts to change."

"And the next bit of the trail is the CPS conference," said Jack.

"Right," Christie took out his time phone. We still have a time signal...What did you say that date was... 31st March... 1836?"

Jack looked at his father's bandages. "Dad – are you going to be OK?"

"I'm fine... it's just a scratch."

"But if we go back to 1836," Angus said. "What about our friend Fenton. He's just tried to kill you and he's still out there, still time travelling around the universe... don't we have to do something about him?"

But they had no time to consider that complication, for at that moment there was a rattle of machine-gun fire from out on the waterfront, followed by screaming and shouting. The Taiping had finally broken through the last of the British defences around the harbour area and they were raising havoc.

Just then, they heard a crash of glass from the bar. "It's time to get going..." Christie said.

There was another loud crash and a fierce-looking Taiping warrior burst into the kitchen. He held a carbine at his side and he wasn't going to waste time by asking questions, but as his index finger twitched on the trigger of his gun, he got a big surprise. The three people at the table in front of him, quite suddenly, just vanished into thin air.

CHAPTER 26
- TRINITY

Cambridge, England, March 1836

They had landed in a small copse beyond the outskirts of Cambridge and they were now walking up King's Parade.

It was a fresh March afternoon towards the end of the Lent term and the street was busy with students and townsfolk visiting the nearby market. Jack, Angus and Christie took a brief detour into a student outfitter to find some more suitable clothing. They passed King's College Chapel – a magnificent stone building, which towered fifty metres into a clear blue sky, eclipsing everything else around it. At each corner of the roof stood a high tower and built into the front elevation was a glorious stained-glass window. As they passed the great building Jack recalled the night they had climbed one of its towers to escape the pursuing Spaniards. He could see the cloverleaf-shaped air holes which they had clambered up and the stone parapet at the top – the decorative crown a good fifteen metres above the roof. He gave Angus a nudge and pointed upwards.

"Remember?"

"How could I forget?" Angus replied. "You nearly got us killed…"

"Saved your butt, you mean…"

They pressed on past the great archways leading into the college quads, and the spires of chapels. It was a bit of a contrast to the Forbidden City and the Summer Palace in China.

"Trinity College – it's up here," Christie said. "This is quite exciting…"

"What," Jack said, "meeting Charles Babbage? Two computer nerds together – I'm sure you'll get on great…"

"Funny," Christie said.

"Yeah – he's hilarious," Angus added. "See what I have to deal with?"

"Think the plan will work?" Jack said.

"Getting in? I think so. The CPS isn't such a big deal right now. It's this conference that will put them on the map and suddenly make them very interesting to the government. If we're right, before tonight, they are just regarded as a bunch of eccentric academics… Once we get in, keep your ears and eyes peeled. Remember what we're looking for – any clue as to how Babbage got hold of the VIGIL device."

"And when he got it," Jack added.

They arrived at the great arched gateway of Trinity College. "Right this is it – everyone ready?"

Christie approached the porter's lodge and a dark-suited porter peered at them suspiciously.

"We are here for the Cambridge Philosophical Society conference."

"Name, sir?" the porter asked, looking at a sheet of paper. "Professor Thomas Christie, Edinburgh University, and these are my research students."

The porter looked down at a piece of paper with some names on it.

"I am terribly sorry, sir, but I don't seem to have you on the list."

"What?" Christie said. "Let me have a look, will you?"

"You see, sir," the porter said. "And I am afraid Mr Babbage is very particular about the guests for tonight… It's a very exclusive gathering."

"Yes, I can see that our names are not there," said Christie, glancing up and down the list. "Perhaps you could get a message to Mr Babbage?"

"Well, he will be very busy preparing for the conference, sir."

"I understand. But if you can give him this," Christie handed the porter an envelope, "I am quite sure that this misunderstanding can be cleared up straightaway…"

"I will do my best, sir."

They waited in the porter's lodge as a messenger was sent scurrying across the Great Court to locate Babbage and deliver the envelope.

A few minutes later he returned, red-faced, and whispered something to the porter, who nodded.

"Well sir, apparently Mr Babbage thanks you for your message and says that he apologises that your names are not on the list. He says he would be delighted to welcome you for drinks with the other guests who are now arriving in the Wren Library."

Christie gave a little bow. "Thank you, sir."

They stepped from the porter's lodge into the Great Court of Trinity College with a fountain at the centre and a chapel to the right.

"What did the note say, Dad?"

Christie smiled and gave them a wink, "Just a little something I thought would get Babbage's attention…"

They passed through the Great Court and the cloisters of Neville's Court, towards the Wren Library, a magnificent glass and stone edifice stretching across the far side of the courtyard. The stonework glowed pink in the late afternoon sun.

"Looks like the CPS has generated a lot of interest for this meeting," Jack observed.

A queue of people were filing slowly into the library for the first of the evening lectures. There was a low buzz of conversation as Christie, Jack and Angus joined the queue.

As they made their way slowly into the Wren Library, Jack noticed a weighty, leather-bound book that lay open on a display lectern just outside the entrance. It was titled Principia Mathematica by Sir Isaac Newton.

Christie caught Jack's eye and smiled. "It's even got the great man's corrections... You know, this library has many more famous books – two of Shakespeare's First Folios for a start... one of those will set you back three million quid in twenty-first century money..."

"I know Dad," Jack muttered under his breath. "I'm fairly familiar with Shakespeare... if you remember."

Inside the library, a row of tall, arched windows ran along each of the side walls and at the far end was a stained-glass window. Rows of bookcases lined a broad central aisle. Chairs had been arranged down the aisle, with a dais and lectern at the front. The audience congregating at one end was growing larger by the minute.

"Astonishing..." Christie whispered. "That's the prime minister, Melbourne. Extraordinary... and he is talking to, well, that is a senior naval officer – must be the Admiral of the Fleet..." Christie's eyes were goggling. "I recognise others from portraits of the time... but look, there's Babbage! He's coming over... someone must have been pointed us out to him. OK boys – here we go..."

Suddenly, Charles Babbage, Lucasian Professor of Mathematics at Cambridge University, inventor of the Difference Engine, a man who was a century ahead of his time, was standing in front of them with a curious look in his eye.

"Professor Christie?" he put out a hand.

Christie smiled, "Honoured and delighted, Professor..."

But Babbage didn't smile back, "I confess that I have never heard of you, Christie, but the contents of your note I found most interesting: 'Energy equals Mass times the speed of light squared...' An unusual hypothesis, that energy and mass are somehow equivalent. Fascinating. Why have you not made contact before?"

"Well, Professor, a man like yourself, it is difficult to get your attention. I heard about the conference... and we had to come. I am sorry we have somewhat thrust ourselves upon you..."

160

"I understand, Christie, it is irregular but I think your ideas are of sufficient merit to warrant a further conversation. You are welcome to stay and we should meet after the conference.

He looked at his chain watch. "But we start very soon, I believe we are all nearly present. We in the Cambridge Philosophical Society have high hopes for tonight. It may not be putting it too strongly to say that I believe we are about to change the future..."

"You could put it like that," Jack whispered to Angus.

"Ahh Babbage – there you are!" A short man in a dog collar scurried up towards them, a glass of sherry in his hand. Jack nearly had a heart attack – Backhouse was much younger than he remembered him, but Jack recognised him immediately.

"Josiah – let me introduce you to these guests, er, Professor Christie from Edinburgh University and, I'm sorry..."

"Jack and Angus. My research students."

"Indeed."

Backhouse put out a hand. "Delighted to meet you. Josiah Backhouse, Reverend Josiah Backhouse."

Initially Jack couldn't work out why Backhouse did not recognise them. After all they had been in his captives, held by the Taiping in Shanghai for a couple of days. But then Jack realised his mistake. Of course, Backhouse wouldn't recognise him. As far as Backhouse was concerned this was the first time that he had met them, but maybe it did explain why, in Shanghai twenty-four years in the future, he had thought he had met Jack and Angus before. Jack hadn't understood it at the time, but he did now. It was one of those bizarre circumstances caused by time travel – as Jack and Angus travelled back in time, so Backhouse was travelling forward, and the unreciprocated recognition that Backhouse had of them in Shanghai was now happening in reverse. It was most peculiar. It was also peculiar, and rather disturbing, that Jack knew precisely the time, location and circumstances of Backhouse's death – defending an armed Taiping steamer from an assault by Imperialists led by a young girl, called Shu-fei.

161

Backhouse seemed a lot more jovial than he had been in Shanghai. "We've come a long way, eh, Babbage?"

The professor seemed slightly uncomfortable in Backhouse's presence.

"If you had not rescued me from that wretched place... six years ago is it now? Well, none of this would be possible," Backhouse said.

"I would request you not to mention such things... particularly in front of our guests..." Babbage replied, tersely.

But Backhouse didn't seem to hear him and chattered on to Christie, "It was strange you know, I remember it so clearly. That foggy night – in London – Babbage, here, my dear old friend, took it upon himself to rescue me. Those people from Harmwell madhouse had found me in the street the day before and locked me up. I wasn't mad, of course, I just sometimes had these... episodes. But since then they have never reoccurred." Backhouse's eyes glazed over. "That's when I found him. I found our Lord. He came to me..."

Babbage was becoming increasingly uncomfortable. "I think we've heard enough, Josiah, I don't think these good people want to hear any more..."

But there was no stopping Backhouse. "It changed me. And cured me. I have never had another episode since. God has been with me ever since and I have made it my mission to spread His word wherever I can. But do you know what I find most surprising?"

"Please Josiah..." Babbage pressed.

"When God touched me..." as he spoke, he turned and looked at Babbage with an awed reverence, "he also touched the professor here. I am sure of it. The great man before you was brilliant before, for sure, but from that moment on, it was as if the professor had been given a new gift from God. He created new ideas for new inventions, new machines, designs... such as you would not believe... all from the device we call his 'Seeing Engine'."

Babbage's face reddened, "I said, Backhouse, that we have heard ENOUGH..."

Suddenly, Backhouse got the message and went quiet. There was a strained silence.

"Now, if you will excuse me, gentlemen, I am going to get proceedings underway… we will talk again," he concluded, giving Backhouse a withering look, "alone."

Babbage marched off, clearly angered by the garrulous babbling of his old colleague

"I apologise, Professor Christie, was it? I do tend to get carried away… I'm afraid my friend Babbage is a bit tense about tonight. The 'Seeing Engine' is very valuable. That is why he is concerned, I suppose. You have to forgive him. But when I am with him I am always reminded of that night. The experience was so profound, you see – I am convinced that divine intervention is the only explanation…"

Christie eyed Backhouse curiously. "Most interesting – and tell me, this was at the asylum you say, Harmwell… in London was it?" Then Christie said, "And when would that have been… exactly?"

"I remember it precisely. The Lord visited me on the twenty-fourth of January, 1830. I awoke the next day only to find that I had been incarcerated in Harmwell Asylum. Babbage and Herschel after they discovered what had happened came to get me out. The time was exactly five minutes past nine o'clock. It was a freezing night. I recall it vividly – there was an unfortunate accident in the carriage as we left… and really from then on everything was different. God had touched me; and for sure he had touched Babbage…" He held out his hands at the great and the good mingling in the Wren Library, taking their seats for the first lecture of the CPS conference," and now, here we are. You will be astonished at the revelations that Babbage and the CPS will present to you tonight. Astonished. They will change the world."

"I see," Christie said. "Most interesting…"

"Have you seen the list of speakers and topics, sir?" Backhouse said, pulling a sheet of paper from his pocket.

"Actually, no. Well, not the latest one."

Backhouse looked surprised, "No? Well, I have it here." He unfurled the paper. It was an agenda printed in italic script. "Look at what we have in store – for a man of science like yourself, it will be a once in a lifetime experience."

Christie, Jack and Angus looked down the list of topics and speakers:

A CONFERENCE OF THE CAMBRIDGE
PHILOSOPHICAL SOCIETY
31st March 1836

Introduced by Professor Charles Babbage,
Lucasian Chair of Mathematics

The Derivation of Logarithmic Tables through the use of the
Mechanical Calculating Machine.

Further Applications of Mechanical Calculations
using the Analytical Engine.
The Principles and Usages of Electrical Energy.

The Principles and Usages of the Internal Combustion Engine.
Powered Flight

The New Sciences – Applications in the Military
and Naval Field

As Christie read down the agenda his eyes grew bigger and bigger. "This is... truly remarkable..."

"As I said, Christie," Backhouse replied. "Babbage has been touched by God... Now we must take our seats – the Professor is about to begin. Quick you must take your seats."

Backhouse ushered them into a row of seats before scuttling away. Once he was out of earshot Christie turned to Jack and Angus. "We've hit the jackpot..."

Jack nodded, "That religious experience Backhouse was talking about – back in 1830 – that's it isn't it?"

"Yes, I believe it is, Jack. The true Point of Divergence. It must be. As Backhouse said himself, from that night on, 'everything changed'."

"It wasn't Babbage being touched by God, though..." Angus said. "It was something else..."

"And whatever happened, Babbage must have been given a VIGIL device on that night when they were at Harmwell Asylum."

"So, we'll have to go back again – to that night and see what actually happens. As you say, Dad, keep following the trail?"

"Right, Jack."

"Guys, don't look now, but I think we've got a problem..." Angus said and nodded surreptitiously towards the door.

But Jack did look and his heart jumped when he spotted a late guest taking his seat in the library just as Babbage strode up to the lectern.

"It's Fenton," Jack whispered. "He's back on our trail. Already."

Christie opened his hands and angled his time phone so just Jack and Angus on either side of him could see it. The light was on.

"Time signal is available. I will set it to 1830, Harmwell Asylum in London and we'll be good to go..."

"What, here... now?"

"No," Christie whispered, "Too many people are too close. We should go outside..."

"Sshhh..." An elderly gentleman in the row in front turned around and hissed at them loudly.

Babbage had just started making his introductory address, "... Technologies that will change the world..."

"We get up and leave, one at a time," Christie whispered.

"... Technologies that will give Great Britain insurmountable industrial power..." Babbage continued to announce grandly from his position at the lectern. "... Technologies that will generate new wealth for all the peoples of the Empire..."

Christie was on his feet. "Excuse me, terribly sorry," he muttered as he squeezed his way down the line of chairs and disappeared from the library.

"You go next, then I'll follow," Jack said.

In a minute, Angus had sneaked out. Then Jack got to his feet. He broke from the audience and marched quickly to the library door following in the steps of his father and Angus. Jack could still hear Babbage's self-congratulatory introduction booming out from the far end of the library, and he couldn't help himself, as he walked to the door, he glanced over his shoulder to take a last look. His timing could not have been worse. At that moment Fenton, who was scanning the room, caught his eye. Jack felt as if he had been caught by the cross hairs of an assassin's rifle. A shiver ran down his spine... he wanted to look away, but he found himself staring back. Initially, Fenton seemed a little bemused at the sight of Jack, but then his brow furrowed. Jack quickened his step, the door was now only a step away – he reached out for the handle but found it difficult to turn with his sweaty palm. His legs wobbled and his stomach churned. Suddenly there was a hand on his shoulder.

"Going somewhere?"

Jack swivelled round.

"That would be a pity, because I think we have a lot to talk about," Fenton sneered in a whisper. "Like how you pushed me off the top of a Zeppelin."

Jack tried to pull away but Fenton was strong, he opened a door and bundled Jack through. Everyone was absorbed in Babbage's speech, so no one noticed the brief altercation at the back of the library. Soon they were on the landing outside. Angus's fist came out of nowhere. It connected directly with Fenton's cheekbone, but Fenton was bigger than Angus and it was going to take more than one blow to fell him. His head came up again, his teeth were gritted and blood streamed from his face. Angus stepped out of the shadow behind the door where he had waited for Jack to leave the library. Jack saw the expression of surprise on Angus's face – surprise that anyone could come up from such a blow. Instantly, both he and Fenton were brawling their way down the library steps, exchanging a series of vicious blows. Jack looked on, horrified, Angus was getting the worse of it and Fenton was using his greater size and weight slowly to gain advantage. They were at the bottom of the stairs now and Jack had to do something. He looked around for a weapon, anything he could use to help Angus. But there was nothing. Then he had a moment of inspiration. There it was. The huge volume on the display lectern next to the library entrance: Sir Isaac Newton's Principia Mathematica. One of the most famous and valuable scientific journals ever written. With some difficulty, Jack picked it up and looked down the stairwell. Angus was in a bad way. Fenton was on top of him pummelling his fists into Angus's face. Holding out the book, Jack took aim and then let it go.

The very same laws so carefully defined and set out by Newton in the large tome itself, caused the Principia Mathematica to accelerate away from Jack's hands and fall to earth at the gravitational constant of 9.81 metres per second per second. The weighty book connected with the back of Fenton's head just as he was raising his bloodied fist before piling it yet again into Angus's face. The book had not yet reached terminal velocity – the distance between Jack and Angus was not yet sufficient – but its momentum was quite sufficient to knock Fenton out cold.

Angus pushed him off.

Jack rushed down the stairs. "You all right?"

Angus groaned, "I thought I was a gonner."

"You look like crap."

"Thanks."

"What's going on?" Christie rushed back into the lower entrance from the cloister and Jack waved a hand towards the prostrate figure of Fenton. "We had a problem with a gate crasher."

"So I see."

Jack gestured at the Principia lying nearby – "But Sir Isaac and I asked him to leave…"

"Can you stand, Angus?"

"Think so…"

"I think we might be about to lose this time signal… come on…"

They touched the time phone and, just as Jack started to get that strange tingling feeling before the Taurus transport kicked in, Angus turned and bellowed at the prostrate figure of Fenton on the floor.

"Mate – you are HISTORY…" And Jack smiled.

CHAPTER 27
- HARMWELL ASYLUM

London, England, 1830

Christie raised an index finger to his lips and the three of them listened intently, trying to catch the conversation between two men who sat huddled in the booth next to them in the Duke of York. The pub was only half full and near their table a log fire was spluttering to life, adding smoke but so far little warmth to the dank air. The three tankards of ale in front of them remained untouched.

Christie had navigated them to Harmwell only an hour earlier and they had taken refuge in the nearby Duke of York, waiting for 9.05 p.m. and the event when, as Backhouse put it, 'everything changed'. He had not gone on to describe the nature of the 'unfortunate accident', but the notion that they might be about to witness something unpleasant had lodged itself worryingly in Jack's mind.

On entering the Duke of York, they had been astonished to see the bedraggled figures of Babbage and another man, whom they concluded must be Herschel, also sheltering from the cold fog outside, holed up in one of the wooden booths at the far side of the inn. Surreptitiously, they had positioned themselves in an adjoining booth and now Jack strained to catch the men's conversation.

"...it is the money, John, always the money. These rumours... that the Engine won't work, has no value, that it is a waste of money..." Babbage said.

"Have faith, Charles. I support you; the Royal Society supports you. You are the Lucasian Professor of Mathematics. Never forget that. I know the Treasury will support you – you will have your money," Herschel reassured his friend. "You have already built part of the Engine… you have shown the way. And your vision…" there was wonder in his voice, "it is extraordinary… a machine that can perform calculations on numbers. A machine that's accurate… consistently. An end to human error. It is revolutionary."

Babbage seemed to appreciate his friend's encouragement. "Thank you, John, I hope you are right." There was a pause before Babbage reflected on Backhouse's predicament. "Trust Backhouse to get himself into trouble again. Locked up in Harmwell Asylum. He is lucky he has friends like us to look after him."

Just then, the door opened and a tall, thin man wrapped up in a black overcoat came in. He spotted Babbage and Herschel and hurried over.

"A dismal night, gentlemen. Can't see a thing out there."

"Indeed. Well, is he there, Simpson?" Herschel said.

"Yes, sir. It is confirmed, Mr Backhouse is in Harmwell Asylum. They picked him up off the street yesterday – he was babbling and incoherent they say – a danger to himself and to others. Apparently, he was talking about having had some sort of vision, some sort of religious experience. I have left the carriage up the street. We can go there now, but I warn you that they are not being very helpful at the asylum."

Babbage and Herschel got up and followed Simpson out into the night.

"Come on. We need to follow them," Christie whispered. "Keep a safe distance."

The street was deserted but there was no risk of Babbage, Herschel or Simpson noticing them – the three men were wrapped up well against the cold and there was a thick blanket of London fog. A little further up the street an imposing building loomed into view and as they got closer Jack noticed that the windows had bars on them. A gas lamp threw an eerie light over the entrance to the building. The three men ahead stopped by the gate and then Babbage and Herschel went through whilst Simpson carried on a little further up the street. Jack could make out the vague shadow of a waiting coach and horses through the mist.

"There!" Christie whispered.

They found a good hiding place in some bushes just beyond the gate, near the steps to the entrance. They sneaked forward and crouched down, melting into the shadows. Jack caught snippets of conversation.

"Well, let's get on with it," Babbage said.

Herschel banged on the door. The noise triggered a cacophony of screaming, shrieking and laughter from inside the asylum. Jack heard a scraping of metal as a hatch was opened. A gruff voice spoke from inside.

"What do you want?"

"We are here to collect one of your patients."

"Come back tomorrow. You are causing too much of a disturbance."

The hatch slammed shut.

Herschel grabbed the knocker, bashed it with all his might against the door and kept knocking, harder and harder and louder and louder. The shrieking and wailing from inside the asylum became more and more frenzied until finally the hatch opened again.

"What is the meaning of this…?"

Babbage was nearly shouting, "We would like to speak to your superior. Tell him that the Cambridge Philosophical Society is here. I am the Lucasian Professor of Mathematics and we have come to release one of our colleagues, Josiah Backhouse… You might wish to add that we offer a modest reward… but if you keep us waiting much longer in this miserable cold it shall be rescinded."

It seemed to do the trick and Jack heard the door creak open.

Babbage and Herschel disappeared into the building.

Christie flashed his time phone in front of Jack, "Nine o'clock..." he whispered. "Whatever's going to happen, is going to happen in five minutes."

But as Jack looked out from their hiding place all he could see was the weak light from the gas lamp reflecting eerily on the fog. It was difficult to imagine how some momentous event was about to happen that would change the future, forever.

Backhouse's words flashed through Jack's head, "unfortunate accident..."

Two minutes later and the door of the asylum opened again. "Here we go – they're out..." Christie whispered.

A dishevelled-looking man appeared alongside Babbage and Herschel. He seemed thinner than Jack remembered him, but it was definitely Josiah Backhouse. The men walked down the steps from the asylum, back towards the gate.

"Thank you again, my friends," Jack heard Backhouse say.

"It might be the last time, Josiah," Babbage said. "I am not sure how long we can keep doing this..."

"I understand, I don't know what happened to me..." Backhouse replied, apologetically. "These episodes... they come upon one and are impossible to control. I am lucky to have friends who understand."

"Indeed. Anyway, it's late and cold and we need to get out of this god-awful place. Simpson has the carriage waiting."

Jack, Angus and Christie watched as the three men walked up the street towards the waiting carriage. A moment later they heard hooves on the cobbles as the carriage set off back down the street, towards where Jack, Angus and Christie were hiding. They watched in dismay as the carriage, ghostlike in the fog, rattled passed them and off down the street.

"They've gone..." Angus said, "and nothing's happened... I don't understand... "

No sooner had the words come out of Angus's mouth than there was a sudden flash of white light. There was a loud thump and then a scream from the middle of the street. The horses reared and the carriage slewed violently before righting itself and disappearing at top speed into the fog beyond.

"What on earth...?" Christie said under his breath, "Look – I think there's something in the street – there!" They crept forward.

"It's a body – someone was hit by the coach," Jack said. Christie knelt down beside the man.

"He's dead," Christie said. "I don't know where he's come from... but that flash could only have been one thing..."

"A time-travel event," Jack said.

"Landing right in front of the carriage like that and getting mown down. Poor guy, he had no chance in this fog."

"But who is he?"

"I don't recognise him..."

Suddenly, Jack saw something lying next to the body. "Look!" he said.

The object was rectangular in shape but with smooth, bevelled edges. Jack picked it up. It was made of a bright, light material and fitted in the palm of his hand. Along the top there were some indentations and on the middle at the bottom there was a circular depression which looked like some sort of button. The letters on the device were difficult to make out in the dim light, but they already knew what they spelled:

VIGIL

"It's a VIGIL smart device, it must have been knocked from him in the impact," Christie said, glancing back up the street. "I think the carriage has stopped up there. They must know they've hit someone. In a minute, they're going to come back down here..."

"That's how they get the VIGIL device," Jack said. "It must be it, Dad, Babbage is going to walk back down here, discover the body and then discover the device. This is the Point of Divergence. We've found it. The end of the trail."

"But then how did this chap get hold of it?" Christie said, "He's not a VIGIL agent. He looks like an ordinary worker."

"If he's a time traveller, he must have a time phone," Angus said, "That will tell us where he's come from."

Christie did a quick search. "Nothing... help me roll him over. Quickly, they'll be here in a moment."

"There!" The unfortunate time traveller was clutching a time phone in his hand.

"Let me check the co-ordinates..." Christie said.

"It says he's come from the future, present day... location... central London. Trafalgar Square." Christie shook his head. "Makes no sense..."

But it did to Jack and the truth suddenly dawned on him. "I know what's happened Dad. Trafalgar Square – that's where I left the time phone when we travelled back to 1940. I left it up at the top of Nelson's Column. VIGIL were planning to send an agent to retrieve it. Something must have gone wrong. I think this guy somehow got hold of that time phone from the top of Nelson's Column, fiddled with it, and ended up being transported back here by mistake."

"Of course – so we're not at the end of the trail. We need to make another jump. Take the time phone, but leave the VIGIL device here for Babbage to find it."

"What?" Jack said. "But..."

"Just do it, I'll explain later."

They crept back into the shadows and Jack looked back up the street. They could hear voices and the noise of the horses. Suddenly, Babbage emerged from the fog. He spotted the figure lying in the street. Babbage put a hand to his mouth in horror and ran towards the body.

"Herschel come here, help me!" Babbage shouted. He looked down at the body and muttered to himself, "This is dreadful."

Then Herschel emerged from the fog.

"Look here, the poor wretch... we ran him over."

"Just when we saw that bright flash," Herschel said. "But I can't explain it, there's been no thunder. Why the sudden flash of lightning?"

Babbage frowned, "Yes, it is most strange. And the man's clothes – short trousers and only a shirt, and his sleeves are rolled up. Like it was a hot summer's day – not mid-winter. A most terrible accident. Go and get Simpson and Backhouse to come and help us. I will search him – maybe I can identify who he is." Herschel disappeared back into the fog to find Backhouse and Simpson whilst Babbage searched the man. He surveyed the area around the body to see if there were any further clues to his identity. Then he saw it. The small shiny object lying on the street. Babbage picked it up and looked at it. The object might have been some sort of mechanical device – but it was engineered in no way that Babbage had ever seen before. He was mystified. He flicked the device over in his hand and peered closer. He thought he could see some letters, but it was impossible to read what they said in the dim light. Later, Professor Charles Babbage, Lucasian Professor of Mathematics at Cambridge University, inventor of the Difference Engine and the father of modern computer science, would discover what the letters were.

However, he would never learn what 'VIGIL' actually meant.

CHAPTER 28
- AT THE FEET OF THE ADMIRAL

Jack had been here before and he hadn't liked it the first time. He stood up against a curved wall of stone. Angus and his father were next to him. They were perched on a narrow platform of stone jutting out from a very tall pillar, high above a city. Jack's feet were close to one of the edges of the platform. The square below contained fountains and four bronze statues of lions, lying down, arranged around the bottom of the pillar. Just above them was a huge statue of a man, which must have been nearly six metres high. The man gazed out across the city. He wore a broad admiral's hat and his left hand rested on the hilt of his sword. The sleeve of his right hand was pinned to his tunic. He had only one arm.

However, there was one important difference from the last time that they had been at the top of Nelson's Column in central London. There was scaffolding built around the tower.

"Repairs going on," Christie said, "or cleaning?"

Suddenly a man dangling upside down on the end of a rope swung into view right in front of them.

"Get me out of this stupid thing!"

"Gordon?" Christie said. "Gordon McFarlane – from VIGIL?"

"Yes, I am, and I'm very glad to see you gents, 'cos, I don't think I can take any more of this."

"What happened?"

"If you help me down, I might tell you. Now, please, GET ME DOWN…"

With great effort, they managed to untangle Gordon from the rope and protective netting. Finally free, Gordon tried to calm himself. "Remember that time phone, Jack, the one YOU left here, back in 1940? It was too much of a risk to leave it up here, so muggins got the job of coming to retrieve it."

"But you got into a bit of trouble..."

"No one reckoned on any cleaning work happening to the column. So the Taurus delivered me straight into that stupid netting on the scaffolding and then I got myself all tied up in that rope and was stuck. Next thing all my stuff is falling out of my pockets..."

"Don't tell us – including your VIGIL device."

Gordon looked sheepish, "Don't tell the boss, I'll get it in the neck..."

"And then?"

"Luckily, there was only one stonemason up here when I arrived – first day of work. He was a little surprised to see me. As I was untangling myself, he picked up my VIGIL device. Then he spotted your time phone on the ledge there... and started fiddling around with that, I told him to leave it of course, but then it powered up, he pressed a few buttons, I don't know, and WHOOSH, he was zapped off who knows where..."

"I think we know..." Jack said.

Christie shook his head in dismay. "Good to see that VIGIL are keeping up their usual high professional standards... But never mind. I think we're at the end of the trail. It's time to go home and fix this mess for good."

CHAPTER 29
- A WOMAN'S TOUCH

"The blood trail is still here from your injury," Jack said, as they stepped from the Taurus transfer platform and onto the gantry.

"I was lucky…" Christie said. "It looked worse than it was."

The Revisionist base was just as they had left it: messy and in need of maintenance. Jack felt disorientated and queasy. His head throbbed, a nasty side-effect of time travel, but he didn't care. He was just glad to be alive.

Christie led them through to the laboratory.

"Where are we?" Angus asked. "I mean, when are we?"

"We've returned to the point just after you followed Fenton Pendelshape and me to the future. And I need to do one thing, so stupid, I nearly forgot."

Christie logged onto his computer and started typing a message.

"What are you doing?"

"I need to contact VIGIL and tell them that if they are going to send Gordon back to retrieve your time phone from the top of Nelson's Column to do it before they start the maintenance work." He finished typing and pressed 'send'. "That should do it – one email saves the world…"

"Gordon going to Nelson's Column – that's what caused all the change? That was the real Point of Divergence?"

"Yes. VIGIL sends him to get your time phone back and from then on it all goes horribly wrong. A chain of events is set off which changes the future. Maintenance work is starting on Nelson's

Column – the first since the war. That poor stonemason gets hold of your time phone, presses the wrong button and ends up run over by our friends in their carriage outside Harmwell Asylum in 1830. He also gets hold of Gordon's VIGIL device which Babbage picks up from the street. Babbage's curious and brilliant mind gets to work and he realises he is in possession of something incredible. Using the app that shows how certain machines and technologies are put together, Babbage and his team of scientists in the Cambridge Philosophical Society start to recreate them. Soon, the industrial revolution has been massively accelerated, with technologies spreading to other parts of the world…"

"Including Backhouse smuggling them to the Taiping rebels in China," Jack added.

"Yes. Backhouse found God just before he entered the asylum and made it his mission to spread the word. When the Taiping rebellion started in China, he found out they were Christians. He wanted to help them. He feels it is his mission."

"So he starts passing secrets to them, stuff which Babbage and the CPS are working on." Angus said.

"And the whole future changes," Christie concluded. What we saw in China in 1860 was when many of these technologies were already taking hold. But what we didn't see was what came later. The Taiping rebels take over Shanghai and then they defeat the Imperialists and take over the whole of China. Then, China becomes a huge and powerful country in the East and soon the whole world industrialises a hundred years before it has in our timeline. The world is hungry for new energy sources. The pace of development is break neck and it is too difficult to stop environmental melt down. Finally, the climate flips. A new ice age. Where we went, 2046, well, it was the end of civilisation. You saw it for yourselves – a dead planet."

"But we've stopped all that happening, right?" Angus said, slightly nervously.

"Yes, Angus, because it hasn't started yet. It all starts when Gordon goes back to retrieve the time phone. I've now sent the message to VIGIL, and they'll pick that up and know to do it at another time when it is safe."

"Will they trust a message from you?" Jack said uneasily.

"They will do their own checks, I am sure. But anyway," Christie sighed, "my fight with VIGIL is over. It is time for me to come in from the cold."

Angus scratched his head. "So are you saying, Tom, that if we go back up outside onto that rock now there won't be all that ice and everything anymore?" Angus said.

"You saw it in 2046 – more than forty years in the future – so no, it won't be like that now, it'll just be like it was when you walked in here half an hour ago. And it won't be like that in the 'real' 2046 either. We followed the trail to the Point of Divergence and we stopped the future changing," Christie smiled, "Simple, eh?"

Angus looked sceptical.

Christie shrugged, "Well if you don't believe me, let's go and see for ourselves."

A few minutes later they were in the lift travelling up through the rock. It came to a halt and they stepped into the upper access passage.

"Remember this?"

Christie took out his access device and pressed a button. They stepped through into the cellar and Christie pointed upwards. "There are the stairs that take us up to the top."

They walked up the spiral staircase inside the lighthouse. Jack remembered the last time they had been there – the air had been icy cold; but now it didn't have the same bite – it was fresh, but nothing like as cold as last time.

"This is it. Remember this door leads onto the lower balcony of the lighthouse – just below the lamp." He threw it open.

When they had looked out from the lighthouse before it was onto a desolate landscape of ice and rock. The sea that surrounded the island, had been completely frozen as far as the eye could see. Now they looked out onto blue-grey waters that stretched out into the North Sea. There was no ice and no wrecked oil rig. It was a bright summer's day, the sun beamed from a cloudless sky and Jack had to squint and then shield his eyes. Hundreds of noisy seabirds circled overhead, dipping and diving into the sea. A mile across the Firth Jack saw the coastline and the great bulwark of Tantallon Castle. Everything was as it should be.

Christie turned to them, "Now do you believe me?"

Jack smiled, "It's good to be back, Dad. It's, well... it's beautiful."

"And no ice age," Angus added.

"Well, no, but in a way – what we saw in 2046 was a warning. In our history, the planet is still warming – because of the way we live. The climate might still flip – just as we saw it – but hopefully we have a little more time to change our ways or fix things before it's too late." Christie paused. "Tell you what – how about we climb up to the top of the rock? The highest cliffs are on the other side from here – they're incredible."

It was a hard climb up the hill path from the lighthouse to the top of the rock. The island rose up from the sea with sheer black cliffs on all sides – except where the old prison and lighthouse stood. Above them, gannets swooped and dived and hundreds more nested noisily all around. There were so many of them they made the rock look white. They crested the ridge at the top of the climb and then the land suddenly dropped away, precipitously. They could hear the distant roar of the grey ocean as it churned away at the foot of the cliffs far below.

"Whoa!" Angus said. "What a view."

The three of them stood silently gazing out to sea. The breeze ruffled Jack's hair and he felt the sun warm his skin. For the first time in a long while he felt happy. There was a sense that it was over. Before their mad trip to China, Jack had believed that his father had decided that meddling in the past to try and rectify humanity's grievous mistakes so that the future might be better was an unrealisable dream. It was a dream that threatened his own family. The risks he and the Revisionists were running had become all too evident through the latest escapade – even though, ironically, changes had happened because of a VIGIL mistake.

Jack's eyes alighted on the far horizon where the dark blue of the sea merged with the sky. In reality, he knew that the horizon was only a few miles away, but it felt like he was gazing into something limitless – a bit like the future itself.

"So Tom, you're saying, well, everything is back as it was... that all that stuff we saw – in Shanghai and in China... and which lead to the climate meltdown... that's just... gone?" Angus shook his head in wonder.

"Yes, Angus."

"And all the people we met... they're gone too... dead?"

Christie shrugged. "Well, in a way, they never existed in the first place. They were never born... so it was impossible for them to die. But remember that in many ways the alternative past that we saw was very similar to the real one. Events, people... in some ways similar, so who knows... maybe some of them existed in China's real past..."

Jack thought about what his father said and he felt a stab of sadness. The people they had met – Shu-fei, Yi, Lai, Captain Fleming – had all been passionately involved in their own lives and the trials of their own times. It was strange to think that the versions of these characters they had met had just been snuffed out, together with their entire world. These people had become friends, and now they were gone.

"How nice... the three amigos all together."

The voice from behind took them by complete surprise. Jack swivelled round and his jaw dropped.

It was Fenton Pendelshape.

He was standing only a few metres away and he had a semi-automatic pistol in his hand. It was pointing straight at Jack.

"Had you forgotten about me then?" he sneered. "You forgot to finish the job... So here I am, and this time you really are going to die. All of you. You have a choice – I can shoot you or..." he stood on his toes to get a better view of the swirling sea below and gave a little shrug, "you can just jump."

"It's over Fenton," Christie said.

"Over? You fool. It's only just begun," Fenton sneered. "Once I have finished with you and taken revenge for my father's life, I will destroy VIGIL once and for all. Then I will be the only one left. I will bring my father back and together we will be omnipotent. We will recreate the world exactly how we wish it to be. We have the power to go to the past or to go to the future. Unlimited power. I will be like a god..." He took a step forward and waved the gun, "So, who wants to be first to die?"

Jack felt that sick feeling of fear sweeping up from his stomach. It was a feeling he had experienced all too often. Fenton waved the gun again and his voice became angrier.

"Come on then, I haven't got all day..."

Something inside Jack just snapped. They had not survived everything just for their lives to be taken by this madman. Jack's fear evaporated and it was replaced by something else. Rage. He darted towards Fenton, screaming at the top of his voice. He saw the look of surprise in Fenton's eyes. But although Jack's move was unexpected and brave, it was suicidal. Fenton's gun jerked in his hand and instantly Jack felt something rip into his shoulder. It was like he had been hit by a car... the pain was excruciating and it knocked him to the ground. He stared up into the sky and felt his life draining away from him. Fenton loomed over him and pointed his gun at Jack's head as he prepared to finish the job.

But Jack would not be the first to die. For at that moment there was a muffled crack. It was the sound of a gunshot, but it hadn't come from Fenton's weapon. Jack looked up to the find the source of the sound, high up on the rock with the wind swirling around. Fenton reeled and put his hand to his chest. A growing dark patch indicated the location of an exit wound from a nine-millimetre round. He dropped his gun and looked at the blood on his hand. After three more steps forward he veered uneasily beyond where Jack lay. His face was etched with anguish, confusion and pain but Fenton staggered on and, in seconds, he was falling from the edge of the cliff and into the hungry ocean below.

A new figure stood where Fenton had been moments before. It was a woman. She also held a gun, and a grey wisp of smoke licked up from the barrel.

The woman spoke, Jack recognised her voice… and then he lost consciousness.

He was lying on a bed and there was a dull ache in his shoulder. He tried to focus on the faces in front of him but we felt drowsy.

There was Angus, his Dad, and… "Mum?" Jack croaked.

"How are you feeling, Jack?"

"But?"

"You were lucky," his dad said. "We've patched you up – you should be fine – but we need to get you to a hospital as soon as we can…"

"Yeah, you've been shot, mate." Angus said in admiration.

Jack tried to pull himself up but he felt a stab of pain run from his neck down his arm.

"Steady…"

"But Mum, how?"

"You didn't think I would trust you boys to stay out of trouble, did you?" She smiled, "Give me a break…"

"You knew we were here…?"

"I followed you here, Jack. You might not know it, but I keep more of an eye on you than you might think. It's a VIGIL thing…" she shrugged and looked at her husband. "OK I admit it, it's a mum thing too."

"The game," Christie said.

"Point of Departure – Day of Rebellion..." Carole smiled, "Your Dad and I wrote most of the algorithms it uses when we were doing our research at CERN. Right couple of nerds we were. Anyway... as you know it developed into something a bit more complicated. It was the start of all our troubles really. But later on, when the program we wrote was built into a huge, bestselling game, well, sometimes I hacked in – you know – just to see how it was going. It's proved useful. When you left the house this morning in a bit of a hurry, well, I suppose I got a bit nosy. I went down to the cellar and I didn't need to hack in at all. There was a rather interesting message from, who else, but my good husband just staring back at me from the screen. I couldn't let that go, so I followed you. Lo and behold – I make an interesting discovery. The Revisionist base, no less," Carole Christie smiled. "And Jack, how many times have I told you to shut the door behind you?" She looked at Christie. "I've got to tell you Tom – you need to sort out your security here... I just walked in. I'm amazed VIGIL didn't suss this place before."

Tom smiled and put an arm around his wife's shoulders, "She's a bit of a show-off sometimes..."

Jack closed his eyes and sank back onto the bed. Despite the pain, he felt happy.

"Don't go to sleep, Jack, you need to get up. We have to leave the base now. We've been talking..."

"Yeah, and we've made a decision..." Angus said. Jack opened his eyes again.

"We've decided it's over."

"What do you mean?" Jack said, his voice weak.

Christie smiled, "Mum's right. Meddling in the past is too dangerous. It's nearly got us all killed... nearly got you killed, Jack. I'm sorry for what I've put you guys through. I'm going to make it up with the VIGIL team..." he pointed at his backpack on the floor, "But I've got the backup here for our version of the Timeline Simulator. I reckon we can use the models to predict what happens in the future. Maybe we can use that to help influence what we do today to make the future a better place... for all of us. We have enough here to do some good... maybe lobby governments... and it will have to be enough."

"But no time travel, right?" Carole said.

Christie gave a little shrug, "No, our time-travel days are over..." he smiled, "Promise."

Jack heard the words and he felt relieved. But there was a tinge of sadness at the same time – that their adventures of the last few months were over. Their mission now would be to keep the reality of the Taurus and time travel a secret.

"What about this place?"

Jack's mum and dad looked at each other knowingly, "Well – it's going to have to go..."

Jack stood in front of the great blast screen of the Revisionist Taurus for the last time. The mighty machine loomed up in front of him and he felt mixed emotions. He could hear the familiar whine of the generators building and the vibrations rising through the floor.

Christie pressed him, "Come on Jack... we need to go now... it's going to go off in under ten minutes. You don't want to be here for that, I can tell you."

But Jack was rooted the spot, mesmerised by the hulking machine as it readied itself – not to send time travellers to the future or the past this time – but to use its own awesome power to rip itself apart.

Christie dragged him away. "Let's go. The energy limiters are off. When it blows the whole complex will be destroyed. There will be nothing left except a few holes deep inside the rock... We need to get down to the sea tunnel where we'll be safe."

Jack was still woozy and his shoulder still hurt, but he allowed his father to pull him away and they headed back through the complex and out to the lift where Angus and Carole waited anxiously.

"What have you guys been doing?" Carole demanded.

"Relax..." Christie said, closing the lift door, "We were just having a final look..." Carole rolled her eyes.

Christie pressed the button on the elevator for the undersea access level which would take them to the tunnel and back out to Tantallon. The elevator set off and started to rattle its way down through the lift shaft. They could still hear the generators which were getting louder and louder – even the metal lift cage was starting to shake.

"Things are hotting up... we got out of there in the nick of time," Christie said.

But no sooner had the words come out of Christie's mouth than the whole lift suddenly shuddered to a halt. Christie frantically pushed the control buttons and then in frustration gave the side of the lift cage a hefty kick.

"What's happened, Tom?" Jack could hear the panic in his mother's voice.

Way above, Jack heard the generators shrieking now. In seconds they would explode. Jack knew that the explosion would rip through the entire complex and envelop the lift shaft. They would be vaporised.

"There's only one option," Christie said.

Jack could sense his father fumbling in the darkness and suddenly a speck of yellow light glinted from his palm.

"A time phone?"

"A souvenir... I took a souvenir..." Christie said sheepishly. "But look, it's got a time signal... And I think it's our only chance..." There was a pause before he added, "We can go to the past or we can go to the future... anywhere you like." Despite the danger, Christie's voice sounded strangely excited.

"Tom..." Carole said, her voice concerned. "What are you talking about? Just get us out of here before the whole place goes up..."

"But..." for a moment it seemed that Christie was going to change his mind.

The pain in Jack's shoulder throbbed and he scarcely had the energy to stand, he felt he was about to lose consciousness again, but he had the energy to say one final thing.

"Home, Dad. Not to the past or to the future. We just want to go home, please, Dad."

In the gloom Jack saw Christie set the time phone.

Suddenly, the air pressure changed. Jack felt as if his chest was going to burst and then there was an ear-splitting explosion. For a moment, the whole lift shaft was bathed in white light. Jack felt the heat on his face and then... darkness.

CHAPTER 30
- ALL IN THE PAST

Jack was lying in a field. He blinked. It was a fine summer's day – perhaps late afternoon. He stared up into a pristine blue sky. Rolling onto his side there was a stab of pain in his shoulder. He winced. Not far away in the distance he could see a white house. It was Cairnfield. They were home. As he came to his senses, Jack noticed that Angus was nearby, pulling himself to his feet. Jack's mother and father were walking towards them. "That was a close-run thing... not quite accurate, but it could have been a lot worse," His father said.

Carole harangued her husband, "Idiot! I can't believe you nearly changed your mind..."

"Just keeping you on your toes..."

"We're home then?" Jack asked.

"Yes – we're home."

"And not in some time warp, or alternative history with cleaver-wielding nutters or a future where the world's dead... I mean, we're in the present...?" Angus said.

"All present and correct," Christie confirmed.

"And no more time travelling, right?" Carole said.

"Right. Next stop VIGIL. I'm handing in my licence and gun. This time for good."

"Well that's a relief," Angus said as he helped Jack to his feet. "Suppose life's going to be a bit boring now... but to be honest, I think history is overrated – I mean – it's all in the past."

THE TAURUS AND TIME TRAVEL

– Some Notes

The Taurus and its energy source stay in one place. In order to move through time and space, the time traveller needs to have physical contact with a time phone, which is controlled and tracked by the Taurus. Time travel is only possible, however, when the Taurus has enough energy and when there is a strong enough carrier signal. As Jack and Angus have discovered, the signal can be as unpredictable as the weather. Periods of time open up and then close, like shifting sands, so that no location is constantly accessible. Then there is the 'Armageddon Scenario', which suggests that, if you revisit the same point in space and time more than once, you dramatically increase the risk of a continuum meltdown. Imagine space and time as a piece of tissue paper – each visit makes a hole in that tissue paper, as if you had pushed through the tissue with your finger. The tissue would hold together for a while, but with too many holes, it would disintegrate. It is dangerous, therefore, to repeat too many trips to exactly the same point and the Taurus will seek to avoid such scenarios. The precise parameters of this constraint are not known and have not, of course, been tested.

BACKGROUND INFORMATION

In Day of Rebellion, Jack and Angus travel back to China in the 1800s. This was a time of great change for China, as the ruling Qing dynasty faced rebellions from its own citizens and military threats from abroad. The notes below give a little more information on the real people and events of the time.

What was the Taiping Rebellion?

The Taiping Rebellion was a civil war in southern China which took place between 1850 and 1864. It was the worst civil war of all time, killing more people than the First World War – around twenty million people. The rebellion was led by Hong Xiuquan, a Cantonese clerk who fell into a trance after failing his civil service exams and came to believe that he was the brother of Jesus Christ. The Taiping movement was unusual in China because it loosely followed the Christian doctrine – which is why it initially gained some support from sympathisers in Western Europe. The Taiping Rebellion was one of a number of insurrections in China at the time, rebelling against the corruption of the ruling Manchu (Qing) government. The Taiping had a formidable army (with talented generals – such as Li Xiucheng – who appears in Day of Rebellion). However, the failure of the Taiping to take the sea port of Shanghai in 1860 – owing much to the intervention of European troops on the side of the Qing government – proved a turning point and the rebellion was finally defeated in 1864. By this point, Hong Xiuquan had already died from food poisoning.

What were the British and French doing in China at this time?

This was the period of the 'Opium Wars', from 1839 to 1860, which were disputes between the Chinese Qing Dynasty and the British Empire over the trading of opium. Instead of silver, the British East

India Company traded the drug with Chinese smugglers who distributed it through China, against Chinese law. Aware that the trade was costing the country money and that there was a growing problem of addiction, the emperor tried to ban it. In response, the British government sent in the military to force a settlement. As a result, the Treaty of Nanking was drawn up in 1842. This allowed for further opium trade, and also the opening of four more Chinese ports to allow foreign trade. It also gave Britain control over Hong Kong. Later, in the Treaties of Tientsin agreed between China and Britain, France, Russia and the United States, China agreed to further concessions including the legalising of opium trade and the opening of ten more ports. These treaties became known as the 'Unequal Treaties' and had a big effect on British Chinese relations for generations.

Did the British army attack Beijing in 1860?

In 1860, to force the Chinese to meet their obligation under the treaties, eleven thousand British troops, led by General James Hope Grant, and nearly seven thousand French, led by General Cousin-Montauban, landed in the north and marched towards Beijing. The Emperor sent ministers for peace talks when the army neared Beijing, however, the British diplomatic envoy, Harry Parkes, together with Henry Loch and a small group of men travelling with them were arrested during negotiations and at this point the talks broke down. At the Battle of Palikao Bridge, near Beijing (known as Peking at this time) Chinese forces met with the Anglo–French army. The Qing army was destroyed as a result, and the Emperor fled. Although Parkes and Loch were released, a number of their group were interrogated, tortured and died. As punishment for the treatment of the prisoners, British and French troops looted and then burned the Summer Palaces near Beijing (including the Yuan Ming Yuan Haiyan – the beautiful palace that features in the game Point-of-Departure – Day of Rebellion and which Jack and Angus also see for real). Looting by occupying armies was a common occurrence –

but the destruction of the exquisite Summer Palaces is now considered a terrible act of vandalism.

Who was Charles Babbage?

Charles Babbage lived from 1791 to 1871 and was a British mathematician and engineer. He was Lucasian Professor of Mathematics at Cambridge University from 1828 to 1839. Babbage designed mechanical, programmable computers more than a hundred years before the age of computing and information technology. In the 1820s he designed and worked on a prototype for his first computer – called his 'Difference Engine' – although it was never completed. He later designed an improved version, called 'Difference Engine No. 2'. This was actually built in 1989–91 using Babbage's plans and it worked! The experiment was carried out at the London Science Museum, where you can still see the Difference Engine No. 2 today. Later, Babbage started designing a more complicated machine called 'the Analytical Engine', which could be programmed using punched cards. Babbage had a wide range of other interests too – he was an inventor, astronomer and code-breaker and even stood for a seat in parliament twice, although he never won.

Who was John Herschel?

John Herschel lived from 1792 to 1871 and was a mathematician, astronomer, chemist and botanist. He was also a pioneer of photography, and his work in this area included ground-breaking developments such as the invention of sensitised paper. He was elected president of the British Association for the Advancement of Science in 1845. Herschel was a friend of Charles Babbage and also influenced the young Charles Darwin.

Who was Princess Yi?

Imperial Yi Concubine, also known as Yehonala and later Empress Tzu-hsi, lived from 1835 to 1908 and effectively ruled China aggressively and ruthlessly for nearly fifty years. She was the daughter of a Manchu captain and because of her beauty she was chosen when she was only sixteen to be one of the emperor's concubines. When she gave birth to the emperor's only son in 1856, she cemented her political power at the Chinese Imperial court, and when the emperor died, she defeated her rivals at court, to become effective ruler of China – even after her son died in 1873. She seems to have been a key mover in China's resistance when Lord Elgin led British and French troops on an attack against Beijing during the Opium Wars and was one of the reasons that China resisted modernisation and change in the later nineteenth century. Soon after her death, China became a republic. The other characters featured in Day of Rebellion, including Shu-Fei, Colonel Lai, and Josiah Backhouse, are fictional.

What is the Forbidden City?

The Forbidden City, in the centre of Beijing (formerly Peking), was built nearly six hundred years ago as the Chinese imperial palace. It was the home of Chinese emperors and the centre of Chinese government. It has nearly a thousand buildings and houses a fantastic collection of artworks from the Ming and Qing dynasties.

What is the Great Wall of China?

The Great Wall of China dates back more than two thousand years and was built to protect China's northern borders from invasion. It is actually made up of several walls that have been built and linked since the fifth century BC. The wall stretches along an arc that more or less follows the edge of Inner Mongolia. It is around 5,500 miles in total and is one of the largest building projects every undertaken. However, the wall did not offer complete protection: the Manchus invaded China from the north in the seventeenth century and went on to form the Qing dynasty which lasted until the end of the nineteenth century.

Did the Chinese really have Zeppelins?

No. The accelerated industrial revolution depicted in Day of Rebellion, caused by Babbage's access to a VIGIL smart device, is fictional, as is the early industrialisation of China. Ferdinand Adolph Heinrich von Zeppelin designed the first airships, which were built and used by the Germans in the early 1900s. Although used in the First World War, airships proved vulnerable to attack and fragile in poor weather conditions. The airships relied for their buoyancy on the use of a lighter-than-air gas. As only the US possessed helium – a rare gas – in usable quantities, during wartime the Germans were forced to use hydrogen, which was highly flammable. In peacetime, however, German airships did clock up many tens of thousands of passenger miles in safety. However, the age of the airship was dealt a death blow in 1937, when a ship called the Hindenberg exploded when landing in the United States – an event that was captured on newsreel film. The description of the Zeppelin in Day of Rebellion is essentially accurate – including the astonishing sub-cloud car (or Spahkorb) which Jack experiences first hand. These were adopted on some army airships to spot bombing targets when the airship was above cloud level. Manning a Spahkorb was cold and dangerous – especially when bombs were dropped from the airship above! However, it was surprisingly popular amongst crewmembers as it was the only place on the airship that they could smoke safely.

What is CERN?

The European Organisation for Nuclear Research, known as CERN, is the world's largest particle physics laboratory and is situated near Geneva on the border between France and Switzerland. Nearly 8,000 scientists and engineers (including around half of the world's particle physicists), work on experiments conducted at CERN – using CERN's giant particle accelerator. CERN also has a computer centre containing very powerful data-processing facilities. To date, physicists at CERN have not discovered time travel, although some believe it may be possible.

ACKNOWLEDGEMENTS

Many, many thanks to numerous friends and colleagues for helping me with the Jack Christie Books, in particular: Victoria Henderson, Caroline Knox, Pam Royds, Phil Perry, Richard Scrivener, Helen Boyle, Anne Finnis, Helen Flynn, Peter Flynn, Jamie Warren, Amanda Wood, Ruth Huddleston, Jayne Roscoe, Rachel Williams, Johnny Lambert, Ruth Martin, Helen Greathead, Will Steele, Stephen Alford, Sara Newbery, Alison Stubley, David Stubley Ann South and many others. Thank you all so much for helping Jack, Angus and myself with our escapades through history.

Most of all I would like to thank my wife, Sally, and children, Annie, Peter and Tom.

Printed in Great Britain
by Amazon

67296786R00118